# Small Town Focus

## A Reed Ferguson Mystery

# Renée Pawlish

# ACKNOWLEDGEMENTS

The author gratefully acknowledges all those who helped in the writing of this book, especially: Beth Treat and Janice Horne. Any mistakes are mine. If I've forgotten anyone, please accept my apologies. If I've forgotten anyone, please accept my apologies.

To all my beta readers: I am in your debt!
Maureen Anderson, Deb Anne, Bill Baker, Greg Ballinger, Suzanne S. Barnhill, Van Brollini, Wanda Bryant, Jan Carrico, Rick Crabtree, Irene David, Karen Dia-Mel, Kate Dionne, Lisa Gall, Tracy Gestewitz, Patti Gross, Barbara Hackel, Gloria Healey, Elisabeth Huhn, JoAnn Ice, Wallace Inman, Joyce Kahaly, Kay, David King, Ray Kline, Cindi Knowles, Maxine Lauer, Lyric McKnight, Debbie McNally, Caroline Molloy, Judi Moore, Becky Neilsen, Gerry Nelson, Ronnie Nelson, Cindi Knowles, Suzanne Nordhaus, Ann Owen, Janice Paysinger, Fritzi Redgrave, Dave Richard, Mary Lou Romashko, Becky Serna, Tracie Ann Setliff, Andrea Shoemaker, Lynn Short, Bev Smith, Albert Stevens, Latonya Stewart, Morris Sweet, Stan Tanner, Jo Trowbridge, Jennifer Thompson, Patricia Thursby, Alice Tileston, Shelly Voss, Sharon Williams, Lu Wilmot, Mike Wynn

# Small Town Focus

# CHAPTER ONE

She got right to the point. "I think my father might have killed my mother."

That wasn't what I'd expected to hear. "Why do you say that?"

She frowned. "I guess that's not the best way to start the conversation." Gina Smith was a petite woman with light brown hair that cascaded down her shoulders and long bangs that covered a high forehead. She was dressed in denim shorts, a striped blouse, and sandals, but her demeanor was anything but casual. She let out a little nervous laugh. "Something odd is going on."

"I'm going to need a little more."

"I know." She sat back, drew in a breath, and let it out slowly. "When I told Willie I wanted to talk with a private investigator, I didn't think it would be so hard to actually do."

I'm Reed Ferguson, the private investigator she was addressing. Gina Smith is a nurse, and a coworker of my wife, Willie – real name Willemena. It was a hot Wednesday morning in late August, and Gina and I were sitting outside at the Starbucks on the Sixteenth Street Mall. It is in the heart of downtown Denver, and since I no longer have an office, it is the perfect place to meet clients: easy to find, public, and I find that sitting with a Starbucks drink seems to relax people, despite all that caffeine.

"It's okay, I don't bite." I smiled to ease her tension.

"What did Willie tell you?"

"Just that you were raised by your dad, you never knew your mother, and you have some questions about your past that you want to talk to someone about."

She sipped an iced café latte, leaving a smudge of pink lipstick on the rim of the glass. "That's true." She fiddled with the glass for a moment and then began. "I'm an only child. According to my father, my mother left us when I was a few weeks old. We moved to Colorado shortly after that, and he raised me by himself."

"He never remarried?"

"No."

"Where were you born?"

"Russell, Kansas, in 1985."

I'd passed through Russell, a long time ago, as I drove east on Interstate 70 on my way to college in Boston. The most I knew about Russell was that former senator Bob Dole hailed from there.

"Has your father ever said why your mother left?"

She shrugged. "He's been very vague, and said that she was unhappy, and she had some problems. I always wondered if it was because of me, but whenever I brought up something like that, Dad would vehemently tell me that wasn't the case. But…" Her lip trembled, and she cleared her throat. "If she'd recently given birth to me, and she was unhappy, how could her leaving not have been because of me? Having a baby is life-changing. I know; I have a son, Ethan."

"How old is he?"

"Eight. He's a good kid. I'm divorced, but my ex has been a great dad, really involved in Ethan's life. I can't imagine abandoning my son like my mother did me. But maybe she had postpartum depression, or something like that. That could've caused her to leave."

"What does your dad say about that?"

"It's a touchy subject, but when I've asked questions, he tells me that the past is in the past, that he loves me enough for both of them, and that I should let it go."

I studied her for a few seconds. "But you've had a hard time doing that."

"Yes. Dad doesn't even have a picture of my mother, let alone anything that belonged to her. And he never even told me her name. I only found out what her name was two days ago. But I'll get to that in a second. I figure I should give you the background stuff first."

I was tempted to interrupt her here, but she was on a roll, so I decided to just let her keep talking.

"It's like he cut her completely out of his life, so she's a complete mystery to me, and that's always made it hard. I have an intense desire to know more about her, to know what she looked like, what things made her who she was, and what made her tick."

"And what made her leave."

"Yes," she said softly. She took another drink, and stared at me with intense brown eyes.

"This is all intriguing," I said, then hesitated. "But I still don't see why you think your father may have killed your mother."

"Let me explain." Two women sat down at a table nearby, so Gina leaned closer to me. "Here's the thing. I was never able to research anything about my mother because I didn't even know her name. But I've looked up Dad, thinking that might help me locate her, and I can't find anything on *him*. He told me one time that he was born in Boston, but I can't find any birth records that might be his, or family history. Nothing."

"How thorough a search did you do?"

She shrugged. "Some internet searches, and I went to some genealogy sites. But with my job and being a single parent, I'm constantly running Ethan somewhere, or taking care of something for him. I don't have a lot of time to do research, and it's not easy."

I mulled that over. "Has your dad ever talked about his childhood?"

"He said he was born in Boston, and grew up near Deerfield, but I can't find any school records, or an old address for him. He worked at a mill in Deerfield, but he wouldn't tell me the name."

"Why?"

She shrugged. "He just wouldn't, even when I pushed him. I looked up mills in that area, but there aren't any." She shrugged. "It's like he only existed when we came to Colorado."

I cocked an eyebrow. "Witness protection program?"

"If that was true, don't you think the government would've told me by now, since I'd be in the program, too?"

"Probably, unless there's some reason to keep you in the dark."

"Like what?"

"I don't know."

Her brow furrowed. "It's like Dad made up his past."

"You've asked him about it?"

"Yes. He just jokes that he was a hell-raiser at school, and then he dropped out. When I pressed him on it, he just told me to let it go. He doesn't ever talk about that part of his life, only things that happened once we came to Colorado."

"Does he have family?"

"If there is, I don't know of them. He says he was an orphan."

"Who raised him?"

"He stayed in an orphanage and then started working when he was twelve, and lived on his own."

"Let me guess, he won't give you the name of an orphanage, and there's no record of any orphanages in Deerfield."

She frowned. "Right. It's possible he stayed at an orphanage in some other city, but he won't say." She let out another big sigh. "I should be able to find something on him, but I can't."

"And all this has led you to believe your father murdered your mother and has covered his past by creating some kind of new identity."

"That's part of it." She turned red. "It sounds preposterous, I know."

I didn't say anything to that, because it did sound unlikely, but I didn't want to offend her.

"There's more," she said.

I took a sip of my macchiato, then set my glass down. "I'm listening."

"A couple of weeks ago, I was visiting Dad and I went into the den. The news was on, and the anchor was talking about skeletal remains of a body that had been found in a field east of Denver. Based on the size of the bones, the authorities thought it was probably a woman. You should have seen the look on Dad's face. He was in shock, just staring at the screen with his jaw open. I spoke to him three times before he noticed I was there, and his face was as white as a ghost. I asked him about the remains, and he snapped at me to shut up." Pain wrinkled the corners of her eyes. "He never talks to me like that. I asked him why the news was upsetting him, and he told me it was nothing, and he changed the subject. Then, the next time I was there, a few days later, I overheard him on the phone. I have no idea who he was talking to, but he said something about the woman in the field, and about it being taken care of, and she was never supposed to be found. He was furious." She tapped the table for emphasis. "He was talking about *that* woman."

"Maybe," I said. "We don't even know if the remains are of a woman, remember? Did you ever find out whose body it was?"

"As far as I know, she's still unidentified."

"As far as you know."

She pursed her lips. "I've been watching the news since then, and they brought up the remains a time or two, but I don't believe they know who it was."

"Does your dad know you overheard his conversation?"

"When he got off the phone, I confronted him, and asked him pointblank who he was talking to, and what the conversation was about. He said I shouldn't be asking questions if I knew what was good for me. That's so unlike him, and I finally got mad back. I said if he was hiding something from me that maybe I should look into it myself. He blew up and said I'd better not go prying into the past, that sometimes things need to stay buried."

"That's an interesting thing to say, given the news about the woman in the field."

"I thought so, too."

I put pieces of her narrative together. "And you think your father had something to do with this woman's death? If it was indeed a woman?"

It took her a long time to answer. "What if she was my mother? What if sometime in the past she came looking for him and he killed her?"

"Why would he murder her?"

"What if Dad kidnapped me, and my mother found us, and so he had to get rid of her? You see stories like that on TV."

I stayed silent for a minute. Gina had observed some odd things in her father's behavior, and I wondered if she realized that she'd made a lot of suppositions, but she had no facts.

"That's a stretch," I finally said.

"I know, but it's possible. I even called the National Center for Missing & Exploited Children, and asked them about any children who went missing from Kansas around 1985, but nothing seemed to be a match. Then I found out my mother's name, but that didn't help."

I held up a hand. "The other night?"

She nodded. "I went over to Dad's, but he wasn't home. I … snooped around. I probably shouldn't have, but because of that woman in the field, and how he responded, I wanted to know if he was hiding something. Turns out he was."

She pulled her phone out of a large purse and scrolled to a picture, then showed it to me. It was a decorative birth certificate, an unofficial form given to mothers when they leave the hospital. It listed Gina Louise Madison as the child's name, and included two tiny footprints and her weight and height. Mother's present name was listed as Marsha Jenny Madison. Where the father's name would've been listed, it was blank. Russell, Kansas was the city and state.

"It was hidden in a box in his closet," she said. "I almost took it, but decided to take a picture instead. I never even knew he had it."

Sadness flashed across her face as she stared at the photo. "That's my mother."

"Does he know you found it?"

She shook her head. "I almost called him later and asked him about it, but changed my mind. If he *has* done something wrong, I don't want to alert him that I'm suspicious. And if this is all in my head, I'd prefer he didn't know what I did or what I was thinking." She sighed. "The whole thing's been eating at me. I can't get past why he won't tell me anything, unless he has something to hide. I even asked him that, and he laughed it off." She stopped and seemed to gather her thoughts. "I want to know what's going on, and I'm willing to pay you to get to the bottom of all this."

I gazed into her pleading face. "Okay," I finally said. "I'll look into it."

Although her dad had certainly been acting strangely, I doubted there was anything sinister behind his behavior, but it would be easy enough to find out, and put her mind at ease.

How wrong I was.

## CHAPTER TWO

I told her my fee and had her sign a contract. As she sipped her drink, I folded the papers and put them into my padfolio.

"I usually talk to Willie about my cases," I said. "Are you okay with that?"

She shrugged. "I don't mind."

"Good." I started firing more specific questions at her. "What's your father's name?"

"John Smith."

I tried not to smirk. "Really?"

She nodded. "What?"

"John Smith? How unique."

She let out a wry laugh. "I know. Try doing an internet search on that name. Everything is for John Smith the explorer. When you get past all that, there are pages of John Smiths. Even when I narrowed my search down, it was impossible to find anything relevant to Dad."

"Narrowed down to what?"

"Boston, or Deerfield, Massachusetts. Things like that."

"What's his middle name?"

"He doesn't have one."

I arched an eyebrow. "Really?" I repeated.

She shrugged. "That's what he says."

"If he changed his identity, what better name to choose?"

She nodded. "I finally gave up my search. I was getting frustrated, and it was taking too much time."

I had my phone out and I started typing her answers into a notepad app. "When was he born?"

"1939. He was older when I was born."

I thought for a second. "Have you searched your mother's name?"

She nodded. "I first searched just the name, and it came up with thousands of results, so I narrowed the search to Kansas, since that's where I was born. I found four Marsha Madisons, and I checked them all. Two were too old to be my mother, one had passed away, and a-nother had married a Madison."

"How did you find that out?"

"I called them."

"I see." I rubbed my chin. "The problem is, they could've been lying to you."

"I guess so."

"And, if we assume the birth certificate is accurate, what if Madi-son was your mother's maiden name, and she's since remarried? Did you find a marriage license?"

"No, but I haven't had time to look very much. Maybe I just missed it."

"Entirely possible. And what if she didn't get the license in Kan-sas?"

She grimaced. "I hadn't thought of that."

"Also, still assuming Madison was her maiden name, and she grew up in Kansas, were there other records, like school information, or family history that included her?"

"I don't know."

"And what if there *was* some kind of conspiracy, or witness pro-tection thing, and her real name wasn't even used on the birth cert-ificate."

She fiddled with her drink glass. "This is going to be hard."

I nodded. "I think so."

She fixed her eyes on me. "There's got to be a way to find her."

I sat back, away from her glare. "There probably is, I just don't want you to get your hopes up, okay?"

"All right, I've been warned."

"And if my search is successful, you might not like what I find."

"I know. I can handle it."

I thought for a second. "What does your dad do?"

"He's retired now, but he worked as an accountant."

I typed that, and then said, "Where does he live?"

"A little east of DU."

The University of Denver is a private university located near Interstate 25 and Evans Avenue. I used to like the surrounding neigh-borhoods, but they'd lost some of their charm after many of the older homes were razed and replaced with pricey custom homes that didn't appeal to me.

"What's the address?" I asked.

"Twenty-one – wait. Why do you want to know?"

I cocked my head. "I need to talk to him."

She shook her head forcefully. "That's not a good idea."

"I can do it in such a way that he doesn't know what's really going on."

"Do you know how mad he would be if he knew I was talking about all this, let alone if he knew I'd hired someone to look into his past and to find out about my mother? And what if you tell him I think he might've done something to my mother?"

"I'm a little more tactful than that," I murmured.

She waved a hand around. "He can't know about any of this."

The two women at the next table glanced at her, and she made an effort to calm down.

"Do you understand how much harder that makes my job?" I asked.

"I'm sorry, but it has to be that way. Dad would –" Her voice broke off.

"What?"

She turned white as fresh snow as she stared past me. I glanced over my shoulder. An older man in gray pants and a white shirt approached the table. Gina flew to her feet, almost knocking her chair over.

"Dad, what are you doing here?" she asked. She was trying not to appear flustered, and it wasn't working.

John Smith studied her for a brief, but calculating, moment. He was average height, with neatly trimmed steel-gray hair, but carried himself with a stern bearing, his shoulders square, stomach sucked in, eyes piercing, and jaw tight.

Gina shrunk slightly from his gaze, and I wondered what was behind that. Was she just surprised because he'd shown up while she was talking to me, or was she truly frightened of him?

He pecked her cheek. "I came for coffee, of course." He glanced at me, his eyes narrow.

Gina gestured at me. "This is my, uh, friend, Reed."

He turned his careful gaze on me as he extended a hand. "John Smith."

I stood up and shook his hand. His grip was firm, and he held it a bit too long, as if to intimidate me. I introduced myself, leaving out that I was a private investigator.

"How do you two know each other?" His eyes dropped to my left hand, and the wedding ring on my fourth finger.

"Reed's a doctor," Gina blurted out. "We're, uh ..."

"I just got off work," I said, then pointed to my empty macchiato glass. "I always need caffeine after a long shift. And I ran into Gina."

His eyebrows went up slightly. "I see." He didn't believe us.

"You don't normally come downtown," Gina said.

He smiled coolly. "I had a meeting close by." He was still looking at me.

"A meeting?" she said. "With who?"

"An accountant." There was something in his tone that didn't sit well with me.

*Now who's lying?* I thought.

"Dad, let's get you a drink." Gina turned to me. "Reed, that ... medical case we were discussing. You should keep at it, at least for a while to see what happens."

"Okay," I said, playing along.

She threw me an edgy smile. "I'd love to hear what you find out."

"You're discussing a medical case?" John asked.

She put a hand on his arm. "A cancer patient who's responding to some new treatment. It's fascinating."

He finally broke my gaze and turned away.

Gina steered him toward the Starbucks entrance. "I'll see you at work and we can talk," she called over her shoulder to me.

"Right," I said.

They got to the Starbucks entrance and Smith held the door open for his daughter. He gave me one final hard look and then disappeared inside. I waited until the door closed, then headed out to the Mall.

I'd parked around the corner on Market Street, and as I walked back to my 4-Runner, I mulled over this new case. I could do a much more extensive search for her mother, but I wondered what I'd be able to find. Both her parents had common surnames – especially her dad – so it would be like looking for the proverbial needle in the haystack.

I had to admit, it was intriguing that Gina couldn't find any information on her dad. What was that about? I doubted it was something sinister. Witness protection only happened in the movies, right? But still.

My mind flashed to the encounter with Gina and her father a few minutes before. She had certainly been shocked to see him, and she had not been very smooth on her feet, which had made her seem guilty of something. That could've explained Smith's distrustful reaction. I shook my head. He'd made assumptions about me, and none of them were good. And I was certain he was lying about visiting an accountant in the area.

"He probably thinks I'm having an affair with his daughter," I muttered to myself as I reached the 4-Runner.

Had Smith been following Gina because he suspected something like that? Was he just an overprotective father, or was he worried about Gina's recent questions about his past? It was too bad he'd shown up when he did. I wanted to know more from Gina, such as how she would describe her childhood. Did she think it was good? Were there any friends or associates of her father that I could talk to without his knowing? Other than the last few weeks, did she get along with her dad? Gina had indicated she would contact me in a day or two, and I'd have to ask her about her dad's showing up unannounced. In the meantime, I had a lot of research to do.

I got in the car, cranked some '80s alternative music – my favorite – and drove home.

## CHAPTER THREE

Willie and I live in a condo in the Uptown neighborhood, just east of downtown, so it didn't take me long to drive home. When I walked inside, she was sitting on the couch, her laptop resting on her lap.

She looked up and smiled. "How did it go? Will you be able to help her?"

"Those are loaded questions," I said. "I took the case, but whether I can find out anything is another story."

"Why is that?" she asked.

Willie is average height, with a runner's body and shoulder-length blond hair. She's a few years younger than my late thirties, she's sharp, and she's a good sounding board when I need to talk through a case. She's even become a frequent sidekick.

I explained the pertinent details of the case. "It's not much to go on," I concluded a few minutes later.

"Huh. Gina never mentioned that she thought her dad might've killed her mother," Willie said. "But she has seemed on edge the last few weeks."

I grabbed a bottle of water from the refrigerator and came back into the living room. "Has she ever talked about her childhood?"

Willie sat back and mulled that over as she played with her hair.

I grinned.

"What?" she said.

"I love it when you do that."

"Focus, babe."

"Right." I cleared my throat and made a show of concentrating on what she was saying.

"Anyway, Gina's childhood. I don't recall her saying much. She mostly talks about her son. I was a little surprised when she asked me if it was all right if she called you. I didn't know that her dad had raised her by himself, or that she had some concerns about him."

"Okay." I pointed at the laptop. "You going to be here for a while?"

She nodded. "I'm looking for a new couch, and deciding on some curtains for this room. Then I'm meeting Darcy for lunch."

Darcy Cranston is Willie's best friend. She lives in a Victorian house across the street that has been converted into apartments. Willie owns the house, and had lived there until the house partially burned down. Then she moved in with me, and the rest, as they say, is history.

"As long as there's no flower wallpaper," I said.

"I already said I wouldn't do that to you. But maybe lots of lace and pink accents. You'd like that."

"Yeah, right."

Once we had settled into married life – all three months of it – Willie had decided that the condo needed some sprucing up, that it was a tad "bachelor." Although I feigned protest, I couldn't disagree. I'd lived here for a long time, and other than my office, I hadn't done a lot of decorating.

"Just don't touch my office," I said.

She sighed dramatically. "Heaven forbid."

"How about dinner tonight?" I asked. "Josephina's?" I suggested, mentioning a nearby Mexican restaurant that we liked to go to.

"I have tomorrow and the day after off, and it'd be nice to spend a little time with you."

"It's a date."

"Then we can discuss paint colors."

I rolled my eyes. "I can't wait."

Her smile remained as I left her to her work and went into my home office. The condo is too small for a true man cave, with a bar, games, a TV and other guy stuff, but my office came close. It's filled with my favorite things, from my collection of first-edition detective mysteries to DVDs of old film noir movies that I love. And I have three original movie posters on the walls: *The Maltese Falcon* and *The Big Sleep*, both starring my hero Humphrey Bogart, and *The Postman Always Rings Twice*, with Lana Turner and John Garfield. Willie had given me the last one as a wedding present, and it was one of the best gifts I'd ever received. She'd put thought into buying me something that truly fit my personality.

I glanced around. "No lace or pink accents in here," I muttered.

I sat down at my desk and logged onto the internet. I first googled for an unidentified body that had been found east of Denver. Even though the story had recently been in the news, I only found a few results. I clicked on a *Denver Post* article dated two weeks ago and read it. It gave me a bit more information than Gina had told me.

The skeletal remains of a human body had been found in a field near Woodrow, a town about a hundred miles east of Denver. A farmer who had been plowing a section of his farm unearthed a skull, and when he investigated, he found other bones. He called the police, who determined the remains were human, but further testing was needed to find whether the remains were of a male or a female. Experts were continuing to search the field for more remains. It was not known at the time how long the remains had been in the field, but it was likely for a number of years. Authorities were treating the case as a suspicious death and were seeking assistance from anyone who might be able to help identify the remains. They did not know the cause of death but were looking into local missing person cases in the area.

I clicked on other articles but did not glean any new information. I was hoping some news agency would've reported whether the remains were male or female, but I didn't find that. Given the amount of time since the *Post* article had been written, I wondered whether the authorities just hadn't determined the sex yet, or they had some reason at this point for not revealing anything more. Fearful that telling the public more might jeopardize their investigation? I pursed my lips. I had one way I might find out.

I picked up the phone, found a number, and dialed.

"To what do I owe this unexpected pleasure?" Sarcasm dripped from the rather gruff female voice.

"Spillman, you sound so pleasant today," I said, matching her sarcasm with my own.

Denver Police Detective Sarah Spillman and I go back a long way. I first met her on a murder investigation, and over the years, I've gained her begrudging respect, although she would never admit that she felt that way. We've reached a point where she was willing to help me when she can. But she had to give me a hard time first.

"What's going on, Ferguson? I'm busy."

"You're always busy, but you always manage to find time for me."

"That's because I know you'll keep pestering me if I ignore you."

"Persistence pays off," I said.

Her sigh was loud in the phone. "Uh-huh. What do you need?"

"Any information about skeletal remains found in a field near Woodrow." I gave her the scant details I had.

"That's it?"

"Yes."

"Do you have any idea of how this person died?"

"No clue," I said. "I just started a case."

"Oh, then I can look forward to many more phone calls."

"I'm not investigating this body, per se, and I'll try not to bother you anymore."

"What do you know about this person?"

"Nothing, I swear."

Another burdened sigh. "Let me check and get back to you."

With that, she was gone.

I put the phone down and turned back to the computer. I typed "John Smith" into Google, and just as Gina had said, the search returned numerous sites about the explorer John Smith. I added Boston to the search, and still came up with thousands of results, which now included John J. Smith, an African-American abolitionist who had lived in Boston. Gina had said her dad was born in 1939, so I tried searching with that criterion. Too many results. I visited some genealogy sites, and checked for a John Smith born that year. Still no luck. I tried a few years before and after 1939. That resulted in a John Smith who had been born in 1938 in Boston, but he'd passed away in 1960.

I next searched for orphanages in the Boston area that operated during the 1930s. Results included numerous sites and references to books that discussed New England's orphaned and abandoned children, and there were even some sites with adoptees looking for their biological parents, but I found very few orphanage names. And nothing about a John Smith, not that I expected his name to leap out at me.

A quick check of the computer clock told me I'd been on the internet for almost two hours. I could see why Gina didn't have enough time for this. The problem was, even if I did find any orphanages, would they still have records available from that long ago? Without more information, or a quicker method of searching, this could take a *long* time. And if I went with a conspiracy theory, and John Smith was a new identity for Gina's father, how would I find out that?

I stared up at Bogie on the *Big Sleep* poster, hoping he would bequeath me inspiration from the great beyond. But he stayed the same, his dark eyes burning with information he wasn't giving up.

"I'll try something else," I finally said, then picked up my phone and dialed another number.

"What's up, Super Sleuth?" my best friend Cal Whitmore said.

Cal is a computer geek who owns his own company that specializes in cyber-security. He lives like a recluse outside the mountain community of Pine Junction in the foothills southwest of Denver. We're like Sherlock Holmes and Dr. Watson, although he is more like the Holmes of our duo since he's way smarter than I am. Yet he has so little common sense, it boggles my mind. He's my go-to guy when I need information that's not publicly available. Cal can access sites I can't – don't ask me how – and he finds information much faster than I could. And although he sometimes gets disgruntled when I ask for help that entails his having to leave his house – he never turns me down.

"What happened to 'O Great Detective?'" I asked. That was his usual greeting for me.

"We need to change it up."

"I think I like 'O Great Detective' better.'"

He laughed.

"Do you have time for some research?" I asked.

"I just started with a new client, but I can fit you in. You on a new case?"

"Yes." I told him about Gina and John Smith, and Marsha Madison. "I've hit a wall with John Smith," I said when I finished. "I know it's a long shot, but see if you can find any John Smiths born around 1939 in or around Boston, or who are listed in orphanages sometime after that. In the meantime, I'm going to see what I can find on 'Marsha Madison.' Oh, can you search on marriage licenses in Kansas for her and John Smith?"

"How's her name spelled?" I told him. Then something occurred to me. "What if Marsha wasn't the correct spelling of her name? Marsha could be spelled 'Marcia.'" I spelled both versions. "And the last name could be spelled differently as well. It wasn't unheard of to have typos on documents, and what Gina had wasn't an official birth certificate." As I talked, I raised my eyebrows at Bogie.

"It's something to check," Cal said. "And I'll warn you, checking on a common name like John Smith isn't going to be easy."

"*Uncommon* words for you, being a hacker extraordinaire."

"It's Clandestine Information Specialist," he corrected me.

"We need to change it up," I deadpanned.

"Not funny." Cal is touchy when it came to being called a hacker.

I heard him typing in the background. I could picture him in his

home office filled with state-of-the-art computers and equipment, man-
uals, and other paperwork. And if I didn't miss my guess, there was probably an empty pizza or takeout box lying around.

"Does John Smith have a middle name?" he asked.

"Not that I know of," I said.

"So just the name, nothing else."

"Right."

"I'll see what I can do."

"Perfect. Thanks."

"You got it, O Great Detective."

I was still laughing when he ended the call.

I had just set the phone down when Bogie's voice said, "Oh, it's
not always easy to know what to do." My ringtone was a sound clip from
Sam Spade in *The Maltese Falcon*. I glanced at the phone. Spillman was
calling back.

"Here's what I have," she said without preamble. "Preliminary
reports indicate the skeletal remains belong to an adult female who was
about five feet six inches tall, with an age range of 25 to 40," she said.

"How long has the body been in the field?"

"From lack of bleaching on the bones, and other forensic evidence
that I'm not going to get into with you, they think about ten years or
more."

"Who found the body?"

She hesitated. "I can't tell you that."

"That's okay." I knew that if I needed to, I could ask around and
find out who it was. People in small towns – and most people in general
– like to talk. "Tell me this. Is he a suspect?"

"They checked on the person who found the body," she was giving away nothing, "but have no reason to think this person had something to do with the woman's death. Right now, they don't have any idea who she was."

"Okay, thanks for checking."

"If you know anything about those remains, you need to tell me," she said.

"I don't, but if I do, I will."

"Fine." She again abruptly ended the call.

I was shaking my head when Willie came into the office.

"I'm leaving now," she announced.

"Okay, have fun. Tell Darcy hi. And remember, my office is off-limits."

"Of course." She leaned over and gave me a kiss. "I'll see you tonight."

"Love you," I said.

"Me, too."

With that, she was gone, just the scent of her shampoo lingering in the air. Right at that moment, I found myself thinking that she could decorate any room in the condo however she wanted to – even my office – as long as it meant she never left me. Then I smiled, brushed that thought aside, and was about to start searching on Marsha Madison when I heard pounding on the front door.

"Hold on," I said as I got up and hurried into the living room. "Did you forget your keys?"

The knocking continued, more urgent.

"All right, all right."

I opened the door, expecting Willie, but Gina Smith was standing on the landing.

"We need to talk," she said breathlessly.

## CHAPTER FOUR

"How did you find me?" I asked.

"Willie's talked about where you live. I didn't have the exact address, but thought I could find it. I was driving down the street and was about to call for your address, but then I saw Willie outside, and she pointed out your place."

"I see," I murmured. I wasn't accustomed to seeing clients in my home, but I stepped aside to let her in.

She brushed past me. "I'm so sorry about what happened at Starbucks!" she said as she began pacing in the living room. "I can't *believe* my dad showed up like that."

"You said he doesn't normally come downtown."

She nodded. "He's never talked about having business anywhere near the mall. He doesn't even like going downtown. He hates dealing with the traffic and parking."

"You think he followed you there?"

"No," she said, a little too quickly. Then she stopped pacing and thought about it. "Oh, man, would he do that?"

"He's suspicious of you, er, us," I said. "Like he thinks we're having an affair, or –"

"I would think he knows me better than that," she interrupted.

"Then why did he show up unannounced?"

"He's worried because I threatened to go to someone for help."

I nodded. "That's what I would think, but you'd know better than I would."

"How did he know where I was going?" she asked, more to herself than me.

I shrugged. She thought about that.

"All I did this morning was take Ethan to school," she went on. "I guess Dad could've been watching the house." She shivered. "That doesn't seem like him."

"What happened after you left Starbucks?"

"What do you mean?"

"Did he follow you here?" *And find out where I live*, I thought but didn't say.

"I don't think so." She grimaced. "You really think he would follow me? I figured it would be better to talk to you right away. I thought about calling, but I really wanted to continue our conversation in person, so I came here."

"You weren't watching to see if he followed you?" I pressed the issue.

She bit her lip. "I walked him to his car and he drove off. My car was the next block down. I left downtown and came straight here. I guess he could've tailed me. Oh, did I mess things up?"

"Don't worry about it," I said. "Tell me what you two talked about after I left."

"He asked again who you were."

I smiled to try to ease her tension. "I'm a doctor."

She snorted. "He didn't believe us, even though I kept to that story. Then he grilled me with question after question."

"Like what?"

"How did I meet you, how long have we known each other, how long you've been a doctor, which hospital you work at, did we meet for coffee often or was this the first time, where do you live."

All questions that could help her dad check up on me. And if he did, he'd find that I wasn't a doctor. But why would he care, unless he was worried about his daughter having an affair, or about her recent probing into his past?

I flashed back to John Smith glancing at my wedding ring. "Did he ask if I was married?"

She shook her head. "That didn't come up. Why?"

"He noticed my ring."

She shrugged. "Maybe he's worried about me having an affair, but didn't want to say."

"I wondered that. But if he thinks I'm someone you're talking to about his past, he might want to stop me from helping."

"I don't know what's going on with him, he's acting so weird." She frowned. "He'll kill me if he finds out I'm looking for my mother." Then her face went white at her words. "I didn't mean ... he wouldn't really kill me." She was questioning that.

"I'm sure you're right," I said. "But he is concerned about something, and until we know what, I'd be careful around him."

"Okay." She trembled slightly, then gestured at the couch. "Do you mind if I sit down?"

"Of course not," I said. "Where are my manners? Would you like something to drink?"

"Water."

I went to the kitchen and grabbed a bottle of water for her.

"Thanks," she said when I returned and handed it to her. She took a big gulp and then looked thoughtfully around the room. "This place is cute, although it is kind of plain."

"Willie's talked to you about redecorating?"

She smiled. "A time or two." Then she grew serious. "I don't know why Dad's so concerned about keeping his past a secret."

I sat down on the other end of the couch. "What was your childhood like?"

Her expression softened. "It was good. It was just the two of us, and he doted on me. Now that I'm a single parent myself, I can appreciate how hard it must've been for him, raising me and working full time. When I was little, he took me to the park a lot, and swimming at a local pool. He was always there for every activity, every game or school performance. The only time I ever saw him get upset was when I asked about my mother, and even though I was just curious, I learned it was better to let it go. And for the longest time, I did. But now…"

"Did you stay with a babysitter when he was at work?"

She shook her head. "I went to daycare until I started school. Then I'd stay with a neighbor after school, until Dad got home from work."

I thought about the look on her face when her dad showed up at the Starbucks. "Does your dad have a temper?"

"Not at all. He's a pretty mellow guy."

"He's never tried to hurt you?"

"Are you kidding?" She was indignant. "He was always good to me."

"Okay." I backed off from that. "Did he ever date anyone?"

She shook her head. "Never."

"Why not?"

She thought for a second. "I don't know. He was busy raising me, and once I went off to college, he seemed to like working and being at home. He's not big on going out and doing things. He likes being a granddad and spending time with Ethan. He goes to Ethan's baseball games and activities, just like he did with me, and he sometimes babysits for me. Otherwise, he putters in the garden and golfs."

"Did you take vacations growing up?"

"Sure. We took road trips, visited national parks and tourist places."

"Did you ever leave the country?"

"No, why?"

"Could you have afforded to?"

"I suppose. We weren't rich, but I'm sure there would've been enough money to go overseas."

"He might not have wanted to if he has a new identity." I pointed at her. "And if you do."

Her jaw dropped. "He would've been worried about being caught."

"Just a thought." I held up a cautionary hand. "But we still have no idea if your dad is who he says he is, or not."

"Wow," she said. "Could he really have faked his identity?"

I shrugged. "Now that I've met him, I'd like to talk to him, and get my own sense of what he's like."

"You can't."

"I'll continue the doctor ruse, and if he thinks we're having an affair, it would give him the opportunity to bring up his suspicions."

She shook her head vehemently. "You can't talk to him."

I crossed my arms. "You're not making this easy."

"No."

I sighed. "What about any friends? Someone who might know if your dad's hiding something."

"How would you make sure they didn't talk to Dad about you?"

I pursed my lips, thinking. "I don't know yet, but I can figure something out."

"He doesn't associate with a lot of people, but he does have a friend, Greg Martinez. They golf together."

"Where?"

She shrugged. "I don't know. When Dad talks golf, I tune him out."

"Does your dad belong to a country club?"

"That's not his cup of tea."

"Where does Greg live?"

"I don't know. I guess I can find out, if you need me to."

"Try," I said. "But I won't talk to anyone before I talk to you."

"Good."

"Who else does he golf with?"

"I don't know."

"Where did your dad work?"

"Trident Accountants. But you can't go there and ask about him," she said firmly. "Not right now."

I rolled my eyes. "Fine. I'll focus on your mother for now."

"Have you found anything on her?"

"I've barely gotten started."

"Oh, right."

"I did talk to the police about the remains found in that field."

"And?"

"It was an adult female who was about 5-feet, 6-inches tall, and she was about 25 to 40. They think the body could've been put there more than ten years ago. They have no idea who it was, but they suspect foul play."

Her brown eyes grew wide. "What if it's my mother?"

"Let's not jump to any conclusions."

She nodded. "You're right." But she wasn't convinced. She took another gulp of water and stood up. "I'll let you get to work. Let me know how it goes, okay?"

"I will."

I saw her to the door and stood on the landing as she walked downstairs and disappeared around the corner. A moment later, I saw her walking down the sidewalk. She got into an older model Honda Accord and drove off. I watched to see if anyone followed, but didn't notice any other cars drive after her. I waited a minute longer, and when I still didn't see any cars, I went back inside.

## CHAPTER FIVE

It was now lunch time. I fixed a sandwich, grabbed a Coke from the fridge, and went back into my office. I cranked the greatest hits of The Psychedelic Furs, one of my favorite bands, ate part of my sandwich, and then got back on the internet.

I hadn't been able to find anything on John Smith, but I hoped I would have more luck with Marsha Madison. If not, and if Cal was unsuccessful in his search, my case would start and end very quickly.

With that in mind, I typed "Marsha Jenny Madison, Kansas" into Google with quotes, and no results came up. So I took out the quotes and searched again. As Gina had said, there were four Marsha Madisons in the state. I checked each one. Two had been born before 1930, and one was deceased, like she'd said. The final Marsha was born in 1947 and lived in Kansas City. That was the right age to be Gina's mother. I spent a few minutes finding this Marsha's phone number, turned down the music, and then called her.

After a few rings, a soft voice said, "Hello?"

"Is this Marsha Madison?"

"Yes, it is."

"Hi, my name is Fenton Hardy," I said, using the fictional father of the famous Hardy Boys, a mystery series I loved reading when I was a kid. "I hope you have a minute to help me. I'm calling from Denver. I'm doing some genealogy research, and I'm looking into my maternal grandmother's side of the family, and I'm related to some Madisons in Kansas, although I'm having trouble finding out much about them. I found your name online, and I'm wondering if you're related to Joe Madison who lives, or lived, in Topeka."

It was total fabrication, just a lead-in to discussing who she was. And it worked.

"Oh, genealogy, that's interesting," she said. "I've never had time to do much of that myself."

"Yes, it's fascinating." Most people like to talk, especially about themselves, and Marsha was no exception.

"Joe Madison?"

"Yes."

"I don't know that name," she said. "Madison is my husband's name, and although I know some about his family, I'm not sure I'm the best person for you to talk to."

"I see. What's your husband's name?"

"Bill. Well, William is his full name."

"Let me check my notes on the family tree I have." I paused. "Do you have children?"

"Two boys. Billy and Troy. Billy's 48, and Troy's 46. They're both married. Billy lives here in KC, and Troy is in Utah."

I did some quick calculations. That meant both boys were born in the late sixties. And Gina was born in 1985. A baby born later in Marsha's life that she gave up for adoption?

"Okay, great," I said. "Just out of curiosity, have you ever been to Russell?"

"Russell, Kansas? Just passing through when we've driven to visit Troy. There's not much there."

"Please forgive an impertinent question, but you didn't give birth to a daughter in Russell in 1985?"

"Of course not."

The reply was quick, with nothing but a bit of outrage in the tone. Not like someone who might've had something to hide.

"You said your name was Fenton?" she asked.

"Yes."

"Why don't you give me your number and I'll have someone on my husband's side of the family call you?"

She was through talking to me.

"Sure." I rattled off a fake number, thanked her and ended the call before she could turn the tables and start grilling *me*.

I sat back, turned on the music again, and sipped some Coke. Unless Marsha Madison was lying, and I sensed she wasn't, she was not Gina's mother. I'd been wrong before, but for the moment, I was going to move on.

I finished my sandwich and began a search of "Marsha," first with "Madisen," still filtering on Kansas, but came up with nothing in a straight Google search. I tried some genealogy sites next, but found no Marsha Madisens in Kansas. I then tried some specialized sites that did a more comprehensive background search. It took quite a while to chug through information, only to return nothing useful.

I got up, stretched for a few minutes, and then sat back down. This was definitely not the fun part of an investigation. Then I tried other spellings of the last name. Still nothing.

"Now trying 'Marcia.' Oh boy, more searching," I said out loud, the sarcasm echoing throughout the office.

I typed "Marcia Madison," and found a Marcia Madison Able, but then found that she was too young to be Gina's mother. I couldn't find anything with the other spellings of Madison, but I wondered if I was missing something. I glanced at the computer clock. After five. I'd been searching online for over four hours. No wonder I was bleary-eyed and cranky. I rubbed my hands over my face, shut off the music, and picked up the phone.

"What's up, O Great Detective?" Cal asked a moment later.

"That sounds better," I said. "More natural."

"How'd your search go?"

"It's been tedious, and I didn't find anything, and I'm worried I might have missed something. *And* I've got more to do, and I'm losing patience." I knew I sounded crabby, but I didn't care.

He laughed. "Yeah, the internet can be great, but it can also be a nightmare if you're trying to find something really specific."

I explained what I'd done so far. "Can you check all the different spellings of Marsha Madison, and see if I missed one?" I asked when I finished. "If Gina was born in 1985, that means Marsha could have been born anytime from 1935 to 1970, give or take a few years, depending on whether she was a teenager or a middle-aged woman when she gave birth."

"And this is in Kansas?"

"Start there, but then how about checking the U.S.?"

"The *entire* United States? That could take a long while."

"Okay, how about states surrounding Kansas?"

"That narrows it down a bit." He started typing. "I'll call when I get some results."

"Thanks. Next time I'm up there, I'll bring pizza and beer."

"As long as I can stay in my home, I kind of enjoy this. It's a break from the usual."

Only Cal would think staring at a monitor for hours was fun. To say he was a homebody was an understatement. He's like Sandra Bullock's character in *The Net*. He rarely goes out, orders everything online – including clothing and food – and has little social life. And he loves it that way.

"Hey there."

I heard Willie's voice call out, and then the front door shut. A moment later, Willie came into the office and saw me on the phone.

"Still working?" she mouthed.

"It's just Cal," I said as I put the phone on speaker.

He grunted. "Just Cal?"

"Hi, Cal," Willie said.

"How are you?" he asked her.

His voice immediately grew cheerier. He loved Willie, and the feeling was mutual. I was lucky in that my best friend and my wife got along famously.

"Do you think you two can break away?" she asked. "Reed promised to take me to dinner."

"Really? He promised to take *me* to dinner, too." Cal feigned excitement, like an enthusiastic date. I could hear his grin through the phone.

Willie put her hands on her hips, but humor danced in her green eyes as she stared at me. "He did?"

"Yeah, pizza."

"Just pizza?" she said. "I'd demand more, like The Palm."

"Hey." I held up my hands. "Quit ganging up on me."

They both laughed.

"I could use a break," I said.

"You might as well," Cal said. "These search results will take a while. Willie, you get first priority."

"Aren't you sweet? It'll give me a chance to share some paint samples with Reed."

"Paint samples?" The amusement hadn't left Cal's tone.

"We're redecorating," she said. "If you want, when we finish here, maybe we can work on your house."

Cal coughed. "I like my place just the way it is."

Willie was grinning from ear to ear. "Uh-huh."

"Have fun at dinner," Cal said quickly. "I'll talk to you two later."

He ended the call, and she burst out laughing.

"You have him terrified," I said.

"He'll never get a date with his bachelor pad."

"Cal date? Are you mad?"

Her smile faded. "I really don't want to interrupt, but could we go to dinner now? I'm starved."

I slumped back in my chair and yawned. "I could use a break." I pointed at the computer. "I'm coming up with zero."

She grabbed my hand and led me out of the room. "I wasn't kidding when I said I have paint samples to look at."

I mustered all the enthusiasm I could, which truthfully, wasn't much. "I can't wait to see what you picked out."

» » » » »

"What do you want to watch?" Willie was perusing DVDs in a drawer in the entertainment center.

"How about a film noir?" I suggested. "You haven't seen *Slattery's Hurricane* yet."

"What kind of a title is that?"

After a nice dinner and margaritas, and a discussion about what color to paint the living room – Willie was leaning toward a neutral tan with an accent wall behind the couch, and I wasn't sure – we were back home.

"Ah, it's not so bad," I said. "It's about drug smuggling and stars Richard Widmark as hotshot fighter pilot Will Slattery and his girlfriend Veronica Lake. It's a rare movie –" That's as far as I got before my phone rang. I checked the number. "It's Cal. Let me take this in the office."

"I'm not in the mood for something so dramatic, but I'll pick out something," Willie called after me.

I nodded as I answered.

"That was a fast search." I slumped down in my desk chair.

"It's still going, but I thought you'd be interested in this," he said.

I sat up straight. "You found a match?"

"Not exactly. You know how if you do a people search, some of the sites will list possible relatives, or people connected to the person you're looking up?"

"Yeah."

"Well, I found a Jennifer Madisen." He spelled the name, and I wrote it down. "And in the list of people connected to her is a Marcia L. Holder." He spelled that name as well. "I did a more thorough search on Jennifer Madisen, and she used to be Jennifer Holder. She married Benjamin Madisen in 1980."

"So Marcia and Jennifer may be related."

"Right. You remember what was on the birth certificate?"

"Marsha Jenny Madison, with an 'o'," I said.

"Correct. Coincidence?"

"In my line of work, I doubt it."

"Exactly."

"Did you look up Marcia Holder?"

"Just a quick search. She has an old address listed in Sagebrush, Colorado, but that's it. No phone number or any other information. But I have a number for Jennifer Madisen." He gave that to me.

"A 970 area code," I said. "That's right here in northern Colorado."

"Uh-huh. Here's the address."

I wrote that down, too. "That's in Sagebrush, too."

"Yep. Another coincidence?"

"Yeah, right."

He laughed. "Want me to do some more checking on either of them?"

"Let's see what the rest of your search results come up with first," I said. "And I'll see if I can get ahold of Jennifer Madisen. I may find out what I need with that."

"Sounds good."

And he was gone.

I dialed Jennifer Madisen's number and waited. After four rings, it went to voice mail.

"You've reached the Madisen residence," a deep male voice said. "Please leave a message and we'll get back to you."

I ended the call. I wasn't prepared to leave a message until I knew that Jennifer was actually at that number. I'd try again in the morning.

"I'm done for the night," I announced to Willie as I came back into the living room.

"Good," she said.

She was lounging on the couch and was already watching *You've Got Mail*, with Tom Hanks and Meg Ryan.

"Oh, a chick flick," I said.

"You'll like it."

"Uh-huh."

I snuggled up next to her, and pretended that I was enjoying the movie, while I thought about Jennifer Madisen.

# CHAPTER SIX

Thursday morning, Willie and I had breakfast together, and while she ran to the bank, I searched on Jennifer Madisen. I found very little, not even another city listed as a former residence. The only thing noteworthy was that her husband, Benjamin Madisen, was the sheriff of Sagebrush. He was referenced in some articles from the Sagebrush Journal, the local newspaper, but nothing particularly interesting. I searched a bit longer, then picked up the phone and tried Jennifer Madisen again. This time, a woman with a shrill voice answered.

"Hello?"

"Is this Jennifer Madisen?" I asked.

"Yes?"

Tentative, probably thinking I was a salesperson.

"My name is Philip Marlowe," I said, referring to Raymond Chandler's fictional detective.

"That name sounds familiar."

Uh-oh. Every once in a while, someone knew the Philip Marlowe character. I barreled ahead so she wouldn't have time to think about it. "This might sound like an odd question, but do you know a woman named Marcia Holder?"

She hesitated. "Yes, that's my sister."

"Do you happen to know how I can get in touch with her?"

"I'm sorry, you said your name was Marlowe?"

"Yes."

She had quickly become guarded. "Why do you want to talk to my sister?"

It was my turn to hesitate. I didn't want to come right out and say that Marcia Holder might be my client's mother, so how much should I say?

"My client would like to speak to Marcia," I finally said.

"Your client? Who are you?"

"I'm a private investigator."

That sound of a phone call dropping sounded in my ear.

"Hello?" I said, then stared at the phone.

That wasn't how I envisioned the conversation progressing. I figured that by telling her I was a PI she might become more reserved, and that was fine. I was going to suggest that she give my number to Marcia, and Marcia could call me. I didn't think she'd hang up.

I dialed the number again, and Jennifer picked up. No caller ID?

"Hello?"

"Mrs. Madisen, please don't –"

That darn disconnect sound. She'd hung up again!

I tried one more time and the call went directly to voice mail. This time *I* hung up on the male voice on the recorder. I set the phone down, wondering why she'd suddenly ended the call. Did she have something to hide? How could I find out if she wouldn't talk to me? I got back onto the internet, and looked up Sagebrush, where Jennifer Madisen lived.

Sagebrush was a little over a hundred miles from Denver, north of Interstate 70. It appeared to be a small farming community, with a dairy plant and other small businesses. I studied a map, and figured it would take me about two hours to drive there.

I sat back and stared at the laptop while I thought through my options. Try Jennifer again? I doubted she'd talk to me. Road trip? Go out to Sagebrush and speak with Jennifer Madisen in person? It'd be harder for her to brush me off then, and a face-to-face encounter would allow me to better gauge her reactions to my questions to see if she was lying about anything. And if Marcia Holder was related to Jennifer, and Marcia was from Sagebrush as well, maybe I could find some other people who knew her. If so, they might know if Marcia had been pregnant in the mid-eighties.

I googled hotels in Sagebrush, and found what looked like a few cheap motels in the town. Then I saw there was a Sagebrush Inn on the western side of town. It looked like a bigger hotel that might have once been affiliated with a better hotel chain. That would work, if I needed to stay overnight.

Just then, Willie came into the office and startled me.

"You look deep in thought," she said.

I nodded as an idea popped into my head. "How'd you like to take a little mini-vacation?" I asked.

"Did you finish your case already?"

I shook my head. "No, I thought we could combine work and pleasure."

"Like when we went to Aspen?"

On a previous case, I'd needed to track down a suspect who lived in Aspen, a small, exclusive tourist town in the mountains west of Denver, and Willie had gone with me. After I'd wrapped up the case, we'd enjoyed a couple of romantic days there.

"Kind of," I said.

"Where to this time? Vail? Breckenridge? Steamboat?"

"Sagebrush," I said.

"Sagebrush? Never heard of it. Oh, is it out of state?"

"It's a small town on the eastern plains."

She frowned. "That doesn't sound very exciting."

"You'll be with me."

"That doesn't sound very exciting," she repeated.

"Oh, that's cold."

She came over and kissed me. "Just kidding. If we can find a hotel with a pool, I can relax there while you're off detecting."

"That'll work." Although I had no idea if the Sagebrush Inn had a pool. I stood up. "Let's get packed and head out."

"Oh, this'll be fun. A quick getaway."

» » » » »

We stopped for lunch in Limon, the "Hub City" of eastern Colorado where five highways and two railroads intersect, then gassed up and moved on. Farther on, we turned onto Highway 59. The drive north was uneventful, the scenery flat, the landscape all around with consisting of farms, ranches, and barren fields. We arrived in Sagebrush around one. There wasn't much to Sagebrush, although it boasted a large grocery store, a Pizza Hut and a few other fast food joints, and some mom-and-pop shops.

As we drove down Main Street, Willie looked around and tried not to appear disappointed. Although the town seemed to be a mix of older and newer buildings, it did not have the appeal of a tourist town. This was no Aspen.

"It's ... quaint," she finally said.

"Uh-huh" was all I could muster.

"Sometimes these old towns have good antique stores," she said hopefully.

I glanced at her. "You want to shop, too?"

"I can't spend the *whole* time by the pool."

"I'll have the car."

"Maybe you won't be that long."

"Then we'll have some nice, quiet time together."

"I like the sound of that," she said.

I soon pulled into the Sagebrush Inn and parked. There were no cars in the lot, and no people around. A dry heat hit us as we got out of the 4-Runner.

"*Does* this place have a pool?" she asked.

"I hope so."

"If not, what am I going to do?" she murmured. "It's too hot to walk around."

We went inside and checked in and, luckily for me, there was a pool. I took our overnight bags and my backpack with my laptop to a functional room with a bed, nightstand, and an older model TV in an armoire.

Willie looked around. "I think I'll go to the pool now," she said as she pulled her swimsuit from her bag.

"Okay. I'm going to head out." I'd brought my Glock, and I strapped on my ankle holster with the gun.

"Will you need that?" she asked.

"I hope not."

"How long will you be?"

I shrugged. "An hour or two? Then maybe we can find a good

local restaurant for dinner."

"Sounds good."

I kissed her and then left.

Cal had given me the address for Jennifer Madisen, but when I'd googled it earlier that day, the map made it look like her place was in the middle of a field. I didn't relish the idea of driving around the prairie trying to find her house, so I stopped at the lobby to talk to the desk clerk.

"May I help you?" he asked.

He was in his twenties, with shoulder-length black hair and a stubble of beard on his chin. He was staring at a laptop, and by the pops and explosions emanating from it, I could tell he was playing some kind of shoot-'em-up video game. He threw me an annoyed look as he pulled himself away from it.

"I'm trying to find a house – or maybe it's a farm – near County Road 15 and Blaine Road," I said. "But on the map, it looks like the road ends before you get to the address."

"You looking for the Madisen ranch?"

*Small town*, I thought. Everyone knows everyone. "Yes," I said.

"Okay, you go north on Highway 59 until you get to County Road 15." He gave me directions, and then said, "County Road 15 continues east, even though it doesn't look like it on the map. It dead-ends at the Madisen ranch."

"Thanks."

He was back on his laptop before I walked out the front door. I drove out of town and followed his instructions. Most of the land around was dry and barren. In ten minutes, I came to County Road 15. I went east, and eventually the dry prairie gave way to green fields. Then I came to an entrance to a ranch with an arched gateway sign that read "Madisen Ranch." In the distance I saw a large, two-story house with a long porch that wrapped around one side of the building.

I headed slowly down the dirt road and pulled into a circular drive in front of the house, then glanced around. The house was white clapboard, with a pitched gable roof, large windows with black shutters, two chimneys, and a three-car garage. A few tall oak trees towered over the house, branches swaying in a searing breeze. No one was around.

I got out and climbed the porch, my footsteps ringing hollowly on the floorboards. I rang the bell and waited. Deep chimes sounded from within, and a moment later, the door swung open to reveal an older woman in a cream-colored pant suit. Not exactly a ranch-wife outfit.

She was tall and thin, with perfectly coiffed brown hair, and an obvious penchant for gold jewelry. A large diamond flashed on her left ring finger.

"Jennifer Madisen?" I asked.

"Yes?" She looked past me to the 4-Runner.

I had to remember what pseudonym I'd used. "I'm Philip Marlowe."

"I remembered who he was," she snapped. "He's that detective from the movies." She surveyed me up and down. "I don't know who *you* are, but I have nothing to say to you."

With that, she slammed the door shut with a bang.

# CHAPTER SEVEN

I was momentarily stunned, and then I punched the doorbell again.

"Mrs. Madisen?" I called out.

Nothing.

I rang the bell again, then pounded on the door and hollered her name, wondering how long it would take her to lose patience and come back out. When nothing happened, I rang one more time, then moved to a rocker on the porch and sat down. I'd driven almost two hours to get to Sagebrush, and I had nothing better to do, so I'd wait her out. She'd eventually have to come out to tell me to go away, and I'd tell her why I was here. Maybe that would get her to talk to me.

After fifteen minutes of rocking, I had built up a sweat, even though I was sitting in the shade. I was also growing angry, wondering why Jennifer wasn't making an appearance, and questioning my own stupid plan.

I dithered about what to do, then finally stood up and was about to ring the bell again when I saw a cloud of dust building down the road. As it drew closer, a dark-colored sheriff's cruiser came into view. I sighed. In my annoyance, I'd forgotten who Jennifer was married to.

"She called the cops," I muttered. At least they hadn't come with sirens blaring and lights flashing. That would've been overkill just to get little ole me.

The cruiser came around the circular drive and screeched to a stop behind the 4-Runner. A big, bald man with a wide chest emerged from the car. He wore a tan uniform, dark boots, and sunglasses, and he put on his campaign hat as he walked around the front of the car. He came toward me in a saunter meant to seem casual, but was clearly not.

"Can I help you, son?" he asked in a deep voice.

Now that he was closer, I noticed a few wrinkles on his weathered face, and I pegged him in his fifties. A bit older than my almost forty. I was also keenly aware that he was bigger than I first thought. I took two steps backward and subtly thrust my chest out, which did nothing to intimidate him.

"I wanted to talk to Jennifer Madisen," I said.

"Do you have some ID?"

I pulled out my wallet and showed him my driver's license, and then my private investigator's license. It wasn't anything official – you don't have to be licensed in the state of Colorado – and he treated it as such, barely acknowledging it. I hoped he didn't pay much attention to the name, since I'd told his wife I was Philip Marlowe.

"If my wife doesn't want to talk to you, nothing's going to change her mind," he observed wryly.

I didn't like that I could see only my reflection in his sunglasses. "Okay," I said. "But it's very important."

He put a hand on the butt of his gun. "What's this about?"

I tried hard not to notice his hand, and stared at my reflection where his eyes should be. "I think I should talk to her about this first."

"Fair enough. If she changes her mind, how can she get in touch with you?"

I still had my wallet in my hand, and I took out a business card that had my cell phone number on it. "She can call me."

He didn't look at it, just took it and slipped it into a breast pocket. "Are you staying in town?"

"At the Sagebrush Inn."

"And you'll be leaving town when?"

"Soon."

The eyeglasses stayed on me for a few seconds. "Good." He gave me a curt nod, dismissing me.

I felt him watching me as I walked to the 4-Runner, got in, and eased back down the circular drive. He stayed rooted in place, and was still there when I reached the end of the road and turned onto County Road 15. Then I finally breathed normally.

As I drove back into Sagebrush, I knew one thing: I had no intention of leaving until I either talked to Jennifer Madisen or knew why she was so intent on avoiding me.

» » » » »

When I got back to the hotel, Willie was lounging in a lawn chair by the pool, reading. She wore a sky-blue bikini, her skin was glistening, and she looked hot – the sexy kind of hot. She looked up when she saw me. "How did it go?"

I kissed her, then sat down in a lounge chair next to her and told her what happened. She was giggling when I finished.

"Not my finest moment," I said.

She closed her book and set it aside. "So you never got to ask her about Marcia Holder?"

"No."

"Did Jennifer and Marcia grow up around here?"

"I have no idea. I could only find this town listed as a place of residence for Jennifer, and I couldn't find anything for Marcia. If they *are* from here, someone will know it." I wiped sweat off my brow and glanced at the pool. "As much as I'd like to change into my swim trunks and dive into that water, I have more to do. Are you okay here for a while longer? I thought I'd ask around town about the two of them."

She blinked at me. "This is a small town, but it's still too much for you to cover on your own. We only have the rest of today and tomorrow."

I grinned. "I'll work fast."

"How about I help you?"

I gestured at the pool. "And give this up?"

"I don't want to be out here too long." She grabbed her book and stood up. "I'll take a shower and then we can start. This'll be fun!"

"Okay," I said. I pulled out my phone and looked up Sagebrush on a map. "It looks like Main Street cuts through the center of town."

"I could've guessed that."

I ignored the jibe, stood up, and showed her the map. "I'll start on this side of Main Street," I pointed at the phone, "and you can take the other side. Work your way west, and I'll go east. We can touch base after an hour or so. Pop in and out of some of the businesses, keep it casual, and see if you can get anyone to talk. And don't draw too much attention to yourself."

"Babe," she patted me on the cheek, "don't worry about me."

"That's a switch. Usually you're concerned about me."

"With good reason. You get yourself into all kinds of jams."

"Ouch."

She laughed and sashayed ahead of me toward the hotel. As I

watched her, I momentarily forgot what I was supposed to do.

"Focus, Reed," I said, sounding a lot like Willie, who said the same thing to me a lot.

"I'll be ready in a little bit," she called over her shoulder. "You want to wait here or in the room?"

"I'll talk to the desk clerk," I said as I caught up to her.

"Okay."

She went down the hall to our room, and I ambled to the lobby. The young desk clerk was still behind the counter, still playing his video game. And I received another annoyed look when I approached. He poked the keyboard with a finger and the sounds of the game stopped, but he kept glancing at the screen.

"Did you find the Madisen ranch?" he asked.

He remembered that. Good.

"I did, thank you." I leaned on the counter. "Unfortunately I didn't get to talk to Jennifer."

"She travels a lot, so maybe she's on a trip."

"Does she have a job that requires her to be on the road?"

He snorted. "She doesn't work."

"You know her?"

"Everybody knows the Madisens." His tone indicated I should've known that.

"Oh?"

"Sure. Her dad's been the mayor here for like, forever, and he owns the dairy plant outside of town. Don't get on his bad side."

"Why's that?"

He shrugged.

After he didn't answer for a moment, I moved on. "What does

Jennifer do, besides travel?"

"I dunno. But she and her old man – he's the sheriff – they got money. I'm thinking of going to school to become a sheriff, if it would get me a ranch like that." He scratched at the stubble of beard on his chin. "You been in their house?"

I shook my head.

"It's nice." He stretched out the word. "They know how to spend."

"I hear there's a sister named Marcia."

He shrugged. "Yeah, I heard my parents talk about her some." He hesitated, as if pondering what he should tell me. "She hasn't lived here in a long time."

"Where'd she move to?" I tried to sound casual, but I was excited. Maybe I'd actually find out something about her.

"I dunno."

And just as quickly, my elation fizzled.

He suddenly focused on me, wondering about my questions. "You're not from around here, are you?"

Boy, was he sharp. Wouldn't that be obvious since I was staying at a hotel? "Correct," was all I said.

"Why all the questions? You a newspaper reporter or something?"

I jumped on the cover he'd just provided for me. "Something like that," I said. "Doing a write-up on small towns and their mayors."

"You could do better," he said.

"Why do you say that? This looks like a nice, small town."

He snickered. "Sagebrush is small."

"But not nice?"

"You live here, you only got so many options." Then he muttered, "They see to that."

"Who?"

His face suddenly paled as he stared past me. I glanced over my shoulder to see Willie coming toward us. She looked refreshed in a pink sundress and sandals.

"Oh, she's with you," the clerk said, visibly relaxing.

"You ready to go out?" Willie asked me as she smiled at the clerk.

The clerk had clamped his jaw shut. He was through talking.

"Anyplace good to eat?" I asked.

"Main Street Café," he said.

"Clever," Willie said.

The clerk gave her a blank look. "Huh?"

"Kind of like a Goofball Brother," I murmured.

Willie smacked my arm.

"Thanks," I said to the clerk. I took Willie's hand and we strolled out of the hotel.

She jerked a thumb toward the lobby. "What was that about?"

I told her about the conversation, and the clerk thinking I was a reporter. "When you're talking to people, see if you can find out anything about the mayor. His name is Holder. Apparently everybody knows him and the rest of his family."

"Anything else?"

I shrugged. "Let's see what we can dig up."

As we drove toward Main Street, I couldn't help but wonder about the clerk's reaction when he saw Willie and, it seemed to me, thought she was someone else. He'd looked scared. Because he'd been talking to me? Why would that be a problem?

# CHAPTER EIGHT

I parked at one end of Main Street, near an insurance office.

"I'm going to start there." Willie pointed across the street as she got out of the 4-Runner.

"Sagebrush Style." I could see mannequins in dresses in the front window. I rolled my eyes. "Are you taking this seriously?"

"Of course. I can shop and talk."

"I'll take your word for it." Like most men, I avoid clothes shopping with my wife, if at all possible.

She laughed as she crossed Main Street and disappeared inside the store. I tried the insurance office, but the door was locked. I moved on, sauntering into a bakery. I ordered a cookie and tried to strike up a conversation with a thin woman behind the counter.

"You like living here?" I asked.

"Sure, it's a nice town." She started frosting a cake.

"Any job opportunities?"

"Maybe at the dairy plant."

"I hear Mayor Holder owns it."

She didn't say anything.

"Is he an okay guy?" I went on.

"Yeah, sure." Not much conviction in her voice.

I tried a couple more questions, but she busied herself with decorating the cake so that she didn't have to pay more attention to me. I ambled back outside and continued down the street.

Half the block was taken up with a feed and grain store, with several pickup trucks parked in front. A few men stood around their trucks and stared at me guardedly as I paused nearby. I was about to poke my head into the store when a flash of neon on the next block caught my eye. I walked toward it and saw that it was a Budweiser sign hanging over the door of McHale's Tavern. A sly smile crept across my face. Willie could shop and talk, and I'd drink and talk. I didn't know many tight-lipped drunks, and I'd bet I'd get some information at a bar.

Cool air hit me as I entered McHale's. I let my eyes adjust from the bright sunshine and glanced around. To the left were four empty booths, and across from them was a long wooden bar. A path between led to a door at the back, labeled "Restrooms." Two men in jeans and worn baseball caps sat on stools at the bar, both nursing beers. A bartender leaned against the back of the bar, watching some kind of fishing show on a TV mounted up in the corner. He glanced over at me and gave me a nod. I walked up to the bar and slid onto a stool.

The bartender sauntered over. "What'll it be?"

"You have Fat Tire?" I asked, ordering my favorite beer.

"Yeah." He reached into a cooler, grabbed a bottle, deftly popped the lid off, and put it down in front of me. "Three bucks."

Not bad, cheaper than bars in Denver. I took a drink and set the bottle down.

"Passing through?" the bartender asked.

"Kind of." I decided to stick with the cover the hotel clerk had given me. "I'm a reporter. I'm writing a story about small Colorado towns."

"This one's small all right."

I took another drink. "I've heard nice things about Sagebrush, that it's a good community, a great place to raise your kids away from the big city."

"Ha!" said one of the guys farther down the bar. He had white hair and a leathery face. His wrinkled hands clutched a beer, and his gut protruded over his Wrangler jeans. His prying ears told me he was bored and dying to talk. "It's strict here, thanks to Mayor Holder. If you cross him, you better look out."

It was clear he didn't like the mayor.

"Watch it, Stan," the bartender said to him. Then he turned back to me. "Don't listen to him. The mayor's a good guy, and he's made Sagebrush a fine place."

A younger guy on the other side of Stan grunted. "I don't care what you say, McHale, Stan's right. The mayor is a mean old SOB."

The bartender – McHale – shook his head. "The mayor's fair, is what he is."

"As long as you play the game," the guy grumbled. He was about my age and stick thin, an old baseball cap tilted back on his head. "You don't play the game, you don't got a job, or anything else in this town."

"Boozer, you lost your jobs due to that." The bartender pointed to Boozer's beer. "Geez, you even have a nickname because of your drinking."

"Maybe so," Boozer slurred, "but you wouldn't have this bar if it wasn't for the mayor." He drained his beer bottle and set it down on the bar with a thud.

McHale cocked an eyebrow at me. "The mayor's all right. The

town's all right."

"Everything's all right with you." Stan guffawed and squinted at me. "You going to write about the mayor, too?"

I shrugged. "I might. It sounds like it might make my story more interesting." And it might help me find out about Marcia Holder.

"He won't talk to the press," Boozer said.

"Holder can be mean, just ask his kids." Stan stared at the bartender, daring him to contradict him. McHale didn't say anything.

"He's got a couple of daughters, right?" I asked.

"And a son." Boozer took off his cap, scratched his head, and then propped the hat back high on his forehead. "I used to work for him."

"Before you lost that job, too," McHale snapped.

"He owns a farm equipment store, down on Tenth Street," Stan chimed in. He finished his beer in a long gulp.

I pulled out a ten and slid it across the bar. "How about a round on me?"

As McHale got Stan and Boozer their Budweiser longnecks, I said, "You think the Holder kids would talk to me?"

"I doubt it." McHale started to put change in front of me and I waved him off. "Thanks. Jennifer, that's his oldest, she lives out east of town. And the son, Toby, he's got a place west of town. But they kind of stay to themselves."

"You got to be in their circle of friends, like rich, or they won't talk to you," Boozer said. He held up his beer at me and nodded his thanks. "Must be nice to have a trust to pay for things."

"A trust?"

"Yeah." He didn't elaborate further.

"What about the other daughter?" I asked.

"Marcia," Stan said. "She's the youngest. She don't live around here anymore."

Now we were getting somewhere. "Where is she now?"

They collectively shrugged.

"No one knows," McHale said.

And just as quickly, I was back to square one. But they were talking, so I kept asking questions.

"Everyone felt bad for Marcia, after that bad business," Stan said.

Boozer frowned. "She never got over it. I knew her in school. She was nice, but after that … she needed to get away."

I stared at them. "What bad business?"

McHale glanced at them. "I think maybe you've said enough."

"Oh, he don't care." Stan waved in my direction. "See, a long while ago, when Marcia was in high school, she got herself in the family way, if you know what I mean. She had the baby, but then someone kidnapped that little girl."

"Poof," Boozer said. "Gone."

I leaned in, trying not to show my excitement. "No one ever found the baby?"

"No," McHale said. He eyed me carefully. "You're better off not talking to the family, and especially about the baby."

"When did Marcia get pregnant?" I kept my voice even.

"Eighty –" Stan started to say.

"That's enough," McHale interrupted.

"Five," Stan finished, and glared at McHale. "Anyway," Stan turned bleary eyes to me. "You ask me, Mayor Holder had something to do with that baby disappearing."

"Maybe I should cut you off," McHale fired at him.

Stan grabbed his beer bottle. "If my money's not good, his is." He pointed a bony finger at me.

"Why would the mayor be involved in the baby's disappearance?" I asked.

"Because he's a mean dude," Boozer said. "And it wouldn't look good for him."

Stan nodded. "And because Pastor Sheehan wouldn't have liked the mayor allowing Marcia to keep the baby after she had it out of wedlock. The mayor was *not* happy about that, and neither was Pastor Sheehan." He propped an elbow on the bar. "Pastor Sheehan is the other person in this town you don't want to cross. You make either him or the mayor mad, you can forget about getting a job or making money around here. They'll see to that."

"You did all right," McHale said.

Stan shrugged. "I played the game, just like you."

Boozer snorted. "And you're still bitter about that."

Stan gazed at his beer and didn't say anything.

"Pastor Sheehan?" I said.

"He's the pastor of the First Community Church." Boozer gulped some beer. "The *only* church in town."

"Well, there's St. Michael's, the Catholic church," Stan said.

"You got a problem with churchgoing folk?" McHale asked him.

Stan held up his hands. "Don't like being forced to go, is all."

"No one forces you." McHale threw him a withering look.

Boozer let out a short laugh. "Yeah, right."

I waited for more, but they clammed up. McHale started talking about fishing, and that turned the conversation away from the mayor and the pastor.

I drank a little more of my beer, but was feeling like the odd man out as they kept glancing at me. I finally slipped off the barstool. "Thanks for your time."

"Good luck with your article," Boozer slurred. "And watch out for the mayor. He drives a black Caddie, so you'll know if he's around."

"Shut up," McHale said to him.

Stan gave me a curt nod. "Appreciate the beer."

"You bet," I said.

As I headed out the door, McHale turned back to the TV, and Stan and Boozer lapsed into silence. I walked outside, my mind racing. Marcia Holder had a baby girl in 1985, and the baby had been kidnapped. It sure seemed like Marcia was Gina Smith's real mother. But how could I track down Marcia to talk to her, if the Holders in Sagebrush wouldn't discuss her? I was also puzzling about the three men in the bar. Why did Stan and Boozer have such distaste for the Holders and Pastor Sheehan, and why did McHale defend them? Did it matter?

# CHAPTER NINE

I walked partway down Main Street and then called Willie.

"Where are you?"

"I just got my nails done," she said.

"Some detective you are," I joked.

"Hey, I've found out a few things."

"Really? Me, too. Why don't you meet me at the 4-Runner and we can compare notes?"

"I'm on my way."

I walked down the next block and as I neared my car, I saw Willie come out of a salon across the street, carrying a bag. She waited for a car to pass, then trotted over to me.

"I bought a dress."

"I can see that," I said as I unlocked the car. We got in, and I cranked the air conditioner, then turned to her.

"Okay, Nancy Drew, spill it." I grinned.

"You may think I'm Miss Marple by the time I finish," she said, referring to one of Agatha Christie's famous amateur sleuths.

I gestured impatiently with my hand, for her to move it along.

She adjusted the vents so the cool air was blowing directly on her, and then began. "So I went into the clothing store first and started browsing. You know, for a small little shop, they had some really nice things. New and used. There was the cutest dress that –"

"Willie," I chided her.

"I'm getting there. As I was looking around, I struck up a conversation with the owner of the store. Her name is Sally and she's lived here since 1960. She told me all about the history of the town, how it wasn't such a great place to live until Alvin Holder moved in a few years after her. He was just a young spitfire, as she said, and he started the dairy plant, which brought in jobs and helped the area flourish." She glanced out the window. "At least as much as a small town can flourish. Anyway, Holder became mayor, and he's really helped make this a great place to live. But it was interesting because I didn't get the sense that she really *likes* the mayor, but she respects what he's done around here. And she talked about how he married a sweet woman named Rita, and they have three kids."

"Jennifer, Toby, and Marcia."

She raised an eyebrow.

"I found out a few things, too," I said.

She reached across and patted my leg. "It's not a contest, hon."

"Ha ha." I told her what I'd gleaned from the men at the bar, ending with Marcia's baby being kidnapped.

"I heard that, too!" she said. "But did they talk about the trust?"

"Just that there was one."

"Apparently Mayor Holder has some kind of trust set up for the kids. They get money from it on a yearly basis – that's the rumor. Sally didn't know *how* much money, but I got the impression it was a lot, since both Jennifer and Toby live pretty high on the hog. Her words, not mine."

"How did you find that out?"

"Babe, I told you, shopping and talking go hand in hand for most women. And when there's a bit of jealousy about money – which I sensed there was from Sally – then that's even more reason to gossip."

"Yeah, but bringing up a trust?"

Willie twisted her hair absentmindedly with a finger as she talked. "I was noticing that some of the used clothes were pretty expensive, and Sally said a lot of it came from Jennifer Madisen. You would have been proud of me, hon. I finessed the conversation around to clothes, then to Jennifer being a Holder, and that led into a discussion of the Holder family, then money, and then the trust."

"Did Sally say anything about Marcia Holder?"

"Like you said, she brought up the baby and the kidnapping, but she doesn't know where Marcia moved to. And she was a little hesitant to discuss anything about Marcia. I even pressed, in a cautious way."

"I ran into the same thing with the clerk at the hotel."

Willie nodded. "It was like she had some strong feelings about the Holders, but also like she was scared to say anything too negative about them, other than the money."

"Hmm," I said. "And yet Stan and Boozer ripped on Mayor Holder."

"They sound bitter."

"Uh-huh." I thought for a second. "Toby Holder owns a farm equipment company here in town. I could pop in there and see if I can get him talking about Marcia. It's interesting, the desk clerk at the hotel didn't mention the brother Toby. But I didn't ask, either."

"Maybe he didn't know about Toby."

"Could be." I drummed my fingers on the dashboard, thinking.

"I've got to find someone who knows where Marcia went."

"I may be able to help."

I stared at her.

"There's more," she said.

"What?"

"After I left the store, I went into the salon to get my nails done." She held out her fingers. "Nice, huh? It's a new shade of pink, called 'Blissful.'"

"You're toying with me, aren't you?"

It was her turn to grin. "I can't help myself. While Kelly – she's the young woman that works at the salon – did my nails, we talked. I got some of the same stuff about the town, how nice it is here. She didn't say anything about the Holders and Marcia, so I brought it up, saying I'd heard about the kidnapping at another store, and how sad that was. Kelly said she'd heard all about it from her parents. Kelly has a baby, a little boy, and she said she couldn't imagine losing your child like that, and how it must hurt the Holders to not know what happened."

"Stan at the bar thinks Mayor Holder might've been involved in the kidnapping."

"Meaning what?"

"He didn't say, and the bartender snapped at him, so he shut up. I don't know if it was just a bitter old man talking, or if there's something more."

She shrugged. "I didn't get a sense from the ladies that Holder was involved. But Kelly did say that her mother always said the whole thing was strange, that the Holders wouldn't discuss the baby, the kidnapping, or Marcia leaving town with anyone. Then she added that if anyone knew about Marcia's whereabouts, it would be Annette Gessler."

"Who's that?"

"She was a good friend of Marcia's. Kelly said her mom used to say that *if* anyone had any information about where Marcia went to, it would be Annette. And yet, Kelly didn't seem to think Annette really did know anything, that it was just part of what people said when they discussed the kidnapping."

"So no one in this town has any idea what happened to Marcia?" I said.

"They seem to be in each other's business, except about that."

"Hard to believe."

"Or they don't want to say."

"Why?"

She shrugged.

"What if Marcia is Gina's mother, and John Smith kidnapped her to keep her from her family and this crazy town? And Marcia couldn't handle it and left."

"If that's true, what's Gina going to think about that?"

"I don't know. I should talk to Annette, to see if she knows anything," I said. "Did you find out where she lives?"

"I didn't want to ask and look suspicious."

"I'll figure it out." I mulled over everything we'd learned. "Did anyone bring up a Pastor Sheehan?"

"Just that he runs a really nice church, and if I'm here over the weekend, I should stay for the service." Her brow furrowed.

"And?"

"There's something that I can't quite put my finger on, but this town gives me the creeps." She shivered.

I agreed. "Remember *Footloose*, with Kevin Bacon? The preacher had so much control over the town that dancing was illegal? It feels a little like that."

She laughed. "Have we entered the *Twilight Zone*?" She started humming the theme song from the show.

"Could be."

"Shouldn't it remind you of a film noir movie instead of *Footloose*?"

"What about *City That Never Sleeps*? Although, that's more about a bunch of people during one night in Chicago who all want to escape their fate for something better. Not so much about the entire city being weird. But it's a good movie, with some great cinematography –"

"Focus, Babe."

"Right," I said. "You want to go back to the hotel? They might have a phone book, and I'll see if I can find Annette Gessler's address."

She nodded. "I'll hang out by the pool again while you talk to her. I'm reading a good book."

"What book?"

"*Web of Deceit*, by Renée Pawlish."

"Never heard of her," I said as I pulled the car onto Main Street. Then I noticed a sheriff's cruiser zoom up behind me. I stared in the rearview mirror for a moment.

Willie noticed. "What?"

"Just wondering if the sheriff is keeping tabs on us."

Willie peered in her side mirror. "Is the sheriff driving?"

I stared for a moment longer. "No, it must be a deputy. But the sheriff could've called someone to look out for the 4-Runner."

"You aroused suspicion when Jennifer told her husband you were Philip Marlowe, and he knows you're not."

"How was I supposed to know things would turn out like this?" I said.

The cruiser stayed with us. I drove the speed limit back to the hotel, and when I turned into the parking lot, the cruiser kept going.

"That was odd," Willie said as we got out of the car.

I gazed after the cruiser until it disappeared in the distance.

Willie was watching me. "I'm sure it's nothing."

I nodded, then followed her inside the hotel.

# CHAPTER TEN

Maybe it was my imagination, but I thought the clerk eyed us warily as we walked through the lobby.

"You're making me paranoid," I said to Willie, thinking the same thing she'd said in the 4-Runner: this town was giving me the creeps.

"Huh?"

"Never mind."

We went to our room, and while she changed back into her swimsuit and prepared to go out to the pool, I searched for a phone book.

"Just like Bogie would've done," I muttered.

I found an old, thin country phone book in the nightstand drawer, thumbed through it, and found Annette Gessler's number right away. That was much easier than trying to find the information online, where more and more sites charged for something as simple as a phone number or address. What was a private eye to do?

"Did you find her?" Willie asked as she rubbed sunscreen on her legs.

I held up the phone book. "I did. She lives on Elm Street. But I don't know where that is, so I'll have to get online anyway."

She stared at me. "What does that mean?"

"Nothing." I tossed the phone book on the bed and pulled out my phone. "Thank goodness for Google Maps." I logged onto the internet. "Elm is on the other end of town."

Willie checked the time. "It's almost four o'clock. You better get going so you miss rush hour."

I laughed. "Funny." I thought for a second. "I'm going to drop by unannounced. If Annette's not there, I may stop by Toby Holder's farm equipment shop."

"So you don't know how long you'll be." She came over and kissed me. "I knew this was a work trip. Do what you need to do and we can get dinner when you're finished."

"I'll see you in a while."

We walked out together, and she headed for the pool while I passed back through the lobby. Sure enough, the clerk was playing his video game – I could hear it – but I still felt as if his eyes were on me when I left.

It took less than ten minutes to get across town, and I was soon driving in an older neighborhood with a variety of house styles. Annette Gessler lived in a white, two-story Victorian home that badly needed a coat of paint. I parked in front of the house and walked up a narrow sidewalk to the front door. I knocked and waited. A moment later a short, plump woman in white shorts and a sleeveless yellow blouse opened the door.

"Yes?" She peered at me curiously through wireframe glasses.

"Are you Annette Gessler?"

"Yes."

I figured I should just use my real name since the sheriff already knew who I was, and if he found out I was still going around town lying to people … well, it wouldn't go well for me. I decided to be blunt and see what happened. "My name is Reed Ferguson. I'd like to talk to you about Marcia Holder."

She was momentarily taken aback. She sucked in a breath, and a hand fluttered to her chest, but she recovered quickly. "Who *are* you?"

"Reed Ferguson," I repeated. "I'm trying to track down Marcia Holder."

"I haven't seen her in decades." She smoothed a hand over her blond hair streaked with gray.

There was something in the way she said it that made me wonder if she was lying.

"Have you spoken to her?" I asked.

"Of course not." She eyed me with a hard look. "I don't know why you're bothering me, but I need to go."

She started to shut the door.

"People around town said you might know where she is."

The door stopped halfway shut. "That's not true," she said. "I don't know anything, and you shouldn't be going around talking about me."

"I'm not trying to," I rushed on, before my opportunity was lost. "I'm a private investigator from Denver. My client is looking for her birth mother, and I'm wondering if it might be Marcia. But I can't find her, and no one will talk to me." I was saying too much, but I didn't want to leave empty-handed.

The door swung back open. Annette looked at me uneasily.

"Please," I said.

She glanced past me at the empty street, alarm on her face. "You'd better come inside." She gestured at me to follow her.

I stepped into an entryway with hardwood floors, an ornate oak staircase, and a fancy chandelier. Down the hall, I could see into a kitchen that obviously had been recently remodeled. A definite difference from the rundown exterior of the house.

"Let's sit in here." Annette went through an archway to the right.

She led me into a living room that was decorated with cream colored furniture, with antique coffee and end tables, and built-in bookshelves along one wall that were filled with knick-knacks and family pictures. She perched on a wingback chair and I sat on the couch.

"Who knows you're visiting me?" she asked anxiously.

"No one." Technically not true. Willie did, but I wasn't going to reveal that to Annette.

She peered out a window behind me, then shook her head. "And who knows about your client?"

"No one," I repeated. I held up a hand. "I mentioned my client – not by name – to Jennifer Madisen, but she wouldn't talk to me after that."

"She wouldn't. The Holders don't talk about what happened."

"What *did* happen?"

Her gaze fell back on me. "You don't know?"

"I know Marcia had a baby in 1985. I heard the baby was kidnapped, and later Marcia left town."

"That's right."

"And I'm getting this weird feeling from everyone I've talked to, that there's something more to the story." I stared at her. "My client wants to find her mother, that's all."

"What if her mother doesn't want to be found?"

"I can respect that, and I can let my client know." I leaned forward. "If the mother is Marcia, I'd at least like to verify that. And she can tell me herself if she wants to reconnect with her daughter."

She pursed her lips, but didn't say anything.

"You were friends with Marcia," I said gently.

She finally nodded. "We both grew up around here. I guess you could say we were best friends, all the way through high school." She gave a little laugh. "I guess that's why everyone in town keeps saying I must know where Marcia is."

"Do you?"

"I don't know as much about things as people think."

"When did she get pregnant?"

"We were seniors."

I thought about what others had said about Mayor Holder. "That didn't go over well with her father."

"No. He could be a bit," she searched for the word, "controlling."

"Who was the father?"

"I don't know."

I cocked a skeptical eyebrow at her. "Come on. You were best friends."

"I'm telling you the truth, she wouldn't tell me. She said she really loved the guy, but he was an older man and she was scared that her father wouldn't like him. She never told anyone in her family that she was seeing someone. And she didn't tell me who he was because she worried that if her father ever found out she was dating someone, and she wouldn't tell him who her boyfriend was, her father would somehow get *me* to tell him. She didn't even tell me she was pregnant until she was starting to show." She frowned. "She was so scared about what her father was going to say, but she didn't want to have an abortion. And then, once the family found out, they wouldn't let her *not* have the baby. Could you imagine what Pastor Sheehan would say if he found out they were considering an abortion? You've heard of him, right?"

"Yes."

"The only other person in this town you don't cross, besides Mayor Holder, is Pastor Sheehan."

"What is Sheehan's first name?"

"Franklin."

"How do you spell his last name?"

She told me, then asked, "Why?"

I shrugged. "I might need to ask him a few questions."

"Be careful."

I nodded. "Was Marcia's pregnancy shocking?"

She snorted. "In a small town like this, of course it was. It was 1985, but around here, that kind of thing wasn't supposed to happen. Not on Pastor Sheehan's watch."

"What happened after she had the baby?"

She sighed. "I don't even know what all happened in the month before she had the baby, let alone after."

"What do you mean?"

"Marcia was about eight months along, and she quit coming to school. When I'd call the house, no one would let me talk to her. They made excuses: she was sick, too tired to come out, that kind of thing. I kept trying until Mrs. Holder got mad at me, and said times were stressful, and that Marcia would call when she could. Marcia finally did, to tell me that she'd had the baby. A girl."

"What was her name?"

"Victoria."

Not Gina, but the name could've been changed.

"Where was Marcia living?" I asked.

"At home." She waved a hand toward the window. "The Holders have a place out on County Road 15, a big ranch. Mayor Holder still lives there, but his wife died a while back. Anyway, Marcia and I talked, and she said her father was furious with her. That was about it because she said she couldn't talk anymore, and hung up. The next thing I heard was that someone had come and taken the baby from the house one night. Just snuck in while everyone was asleep and took the baby from Marcia's room. Marcia was devastated. Her father finally let me come out and visit her, and she was like a zombie, hardly saying anything to me. Her world was completely ruined." She glanced over at the family pictures on the shelves. "I can understand. To lose your child like that, it must've been just awful."

I thought back to what Stan had said. "Do you think Mayor Holder had anything to do with the baby's disappearance?"

"No, of course not," she said, but there was enough doubt in her tone to make me think she'd considered that very thing herself.

"Was the mayor hiding something?"

"I don't know," she said softly. "I've wondered about that kidnapping. Something didn't seem right about their story."

"Like what?"

"One, that Marcia slept through it all." She shrugged. "And … I don't know."

"What happened next?"

"There was a search. The sheriff worked the case for a long time, and I heard the Holders paid people to look for the kidnappers, but the baby was gone. Then life went on. Everyone worried about their kids, but eventually things settled down."

"Was Jennifer married to the sheriff at that time?"

"Ben wasn't the sheriff at that time, but yes, she'd been married to him for several years." She drew in a breath and let it out in a hiss. "Marcia withdrew from the public eye, and she wouldn't talk to me. Then one day I got a call from her. She said she was moving away."

"Where to?"

"She wouldn't tell me."

I threw her another doubtful look.

"She was scared of her father," she protested. "She wasn't supposed to tell anyone what was going on, but she wanted me to know. She said she was sorry about what had happened between us. She wanted me to know she never meant to hurt me, and that maybe one day she would get in touch with me. And she made me promise not to tell anyone what she said." She stared at me. "Up until now, I never have. Not even to my husband or kids."

"Why are you telling me?"

She didn't say anything for a long time. "I thought I'd moved on. I had my own family, and you get busy with things. Up until you came here, I thought I'd let it go. And in this town, you don't challenge people, especially the Holders, so I never said anything to anyone." She sighed again. "But if Marcia might be able to see her daughter again…"

"Do you know where Marcia is?"

She looked away.

"Please," I said. "I won't tell anyone that we've spoken."

Her lower lip trembled and tears came into her eyes. She brushed them away. "She moved to Denver."

"She told you that?"

"Yes."

"Where in Denver? There's no address associated with her name."

"I don't think she had a job. She was going to live off the trust."

"So the trust paid her bills?"

"I don't know how it all works. You'd have to ask her, or Mayor Holder."

"Somehow I don't think he's going to talk to me."

She scoffed. "You're right about that."

"You don't have a specific address for her?" I pressed.

"I don't even know if she's still in Denver. She could've moved away, or died." Her voice caught. "I haven't talked to her in thirty years. But if your client really is Marcia's daughter..." She started to cry. "I shouldn't be telling you this." She wiped her eyes.

I gave her a moment to collect herself, and then asked, "Do you have a picture of Marcia?"

She nodded, then got up and left the room. She returned a minute later with an old yearbook. "I've kept this silly thing all these years." She thumbed through to a page, then handed it to me. "That's Marcia."

I looked at a small picture of a woman with long brown hair and bangs that covered a high forehead. She wore a big smile, and she was pretty, in an awkward kind of way – like so many of us in high school. I closed the book and handed it back to her.

"Why is everybody so closed-mouthed about Marcia and the baby?" I asked.

"I don't know."

"Is everyone scared of the Holders?"

"Could be," she said noncommittally. Then she glanced at a wall clock. "I think you better go. My husband will be home soon. He works at Toby Holder's store, and it wouldn't be good if my husband ever mentioned you to Toby."

"Your husband doesn't know who I am."

"They have ways of finding out things, and I've already risked enough."

I stood up. "I really appreciate your time."

"Don't tell anyone we talked."

"I won't," I said as she led me to the front door. I stepped outside. "Do you want me to let you know what I find out?"

She hesitated and looked around. "It's best that you don't contact me."

I could almost feel the fear emanating from her. "All right."

She closed the door. As I walked back to the 4-Runner, I wondered what kind of person could create that much anxiety in her.

# CHAPTER ELEVEN

When I got back to the hotel, the young clerk had been replaced by an older man in a blue suit and wrinkled white shirt. He stared at me as I crossed the lobby. I waved and he gave me a blank look. I gave him a smile, but got nothing as I headed down the hall to the back of the building. I went outside where Willie was poolside, relaxing on a lawn chair.

"You weren't gone that long," she said as she looked up from her book.

I grinned. "Rush hour was light."

She laughed. "What'd you find out?"

"Marcia Holder moved from here to Denver in 1985, but Annette doesn't know if Marcia is still there, or if she's even alive, for that matter."

"Did Annette have an address for her in Denver?"

I shook my head. "And I don't, either. Annette thought that Marcia was living off the family trust, which would explain why nothing came up in a name search on Marcia Holder."

She sat up. "Do you have the trust name?"

"Nope." I glanced at the empty pool. "Do you want to stay a while longer? Or overnight? We paid for the room."

"You don't want to head back to Denver now?"

I shrugged. "I have to see if I can find Marcia through the trust, and I can do some internet searching with my laptop here."

"Well, we did pay for the room."

"And I owe you a dinner. I could take you to the Main Street Café."

"Oh, that sounds so romantic."

"Are you hungry now?"

She shook her head. "How about I stay out here for a while longer, and give you time to do some research? I'll take a quick dip in the pool and we can go."

"That'll work."

I kissed her and went to our room. I took my laptop out of my backpack, booted it up, logged on to the hotel's Wi-Fi, and got on the internet. I spent a while trying to find something on a Holder trust, but I came up empty. I did learn that because of privacy laws, banks and attorneys wouldn't provide me with any information even if I did have the name of the trust. This called for the big guns, so I grabbed my phone and called Cal.

"Did you find Jennifer Madisen?" he asked in place of a greeting.

"I did, but I didn't get to talk to her."

I told him about Jennifer and her sheriff husband, and he was howling when I finished.

"Oh, that's too funny."

"It may not have been my finest hour, but persistence pays off. After an afternoon of chatting up the town folk, I found out Marcia Holder may be living in Denver."

"But you're not sure."

"Right. Can you check on Alvin Holder and his family, and see if you can find a trust that might be paying Marcia's bills?"

"Ah, if the trust is paying, she doesn't show up on any White Pages searches."

"Right again."

"I've got something I need to finish first. If I get back to you tomorrow, will that work?"

"Sure. Willie and I are going to spend the night here."

"In Sagebrush? How romantic."

"That's what she said."

"I'll call you tomorrow." As usual, he was laughing when he ended the call.

I was just getting back on the computer when Willie strolled into the room.

"Do you want to go to dinner now?" she asked.

"Sure."

"Let me change clothes and we can go."

"Sounds good."

She went into the bathroom and I heard the sink running as I began a search on Alvin Holder. There was a nice profile about him on the official Sagebrush city site, but other than that, I didn't find much. By the time I finished, Willie was in the same pink sundress and sandals as before. And she looked just as cute as before.

"Ready?" I stood up, put my laptop in my backpack and set it on a chair in the corner, then took her hand.

"I hope this restaurant has good food," she said.

"Me, too."

» » » » »

The café did have good food, and shortly after we ordered, I was diving into a thick, juicy steak while Willie started on a chicken salad. When our server – a busty woman with a wide smile – came to check on us, I asked her about Sagebrush.

"It's a nice town," she said, echoing what Willie and I'd heard before.

"I hear that's due to Mayor Holder," Willie said before I had a chance to respond.

The waitress nodded. "Yes, he's been around forever." There was an odd reluctance in her tone.

"I hear you don't want to get on his bad side," I added.

"I, uh, excuse me." The waitress tittered nervously and walked away.

Willie pursed her lips. "See how everyone acts when you bring up Mayor Holder?"

"Uh-huh," I said.

We finished our meal, both keenly aware of the sly gazes from the other people in the café.

"You think it's because we're strangers in town?" Willie murmured as we lingered over a glass of surprisingly good wine after our meal.

I shrugged. "Probably."

"Maybe they're aliens and they're plotting how to take over our bodies."

"Is that from the book you were reading?"

She giggled. "No."

We finally left and walked around town for a bit. Dusk was settling in as we drove back to the hotel. The night clerk was as unfriendly as before, barely acknowledging us as we walked through the lobby.

"Does he make everyone feel that welcome?" Willie whispered.

"I think we're the only ones here," I said. "The parking lot's empty."

We strolled down the hall to our room. I unlocked the door and we went inside.

"Oh, I feel good," Willie said as she stretched out on the bed. She crooked a finger at me. "Come over here."

I grinned, sat down, and took off my ankle holster and started to put it in my backpack. Then I stopped short.

"What?" she asked.

I stared at my backpack. "Did you move that?"

Willie frowned. "I didn't touch it."

"You sure?"

"Of course."

I held up a hand. "I was just asking." I went to the chair, opened the backpack, and peered inside.

Willie slid off the bed. "What's the matter?"

I pointed at my laptop. "I think someone's been messing with my bag. It's not been put back right."

She glanced around, then studied her overnight bag. "That may have been moved."

I pulled out my laptop and booted it up. The password screen came up. "No one could've gotten onto it."

"Unless they're like Cal."

"Good point," I murmured.

I moved around the room, and as I passed by the window, I noticed a dark-colored sedan in the parking lot. I studied it in the gloomy light.

Someone was sitting in the driver's seat, and it appeared that he – or she – had binoculars trained on our window.

"Stay here." I whirled around and quickly crossed the room.

"Reed!" Willie called after me, but I was out the door.

I ran down the hall and through the lobby. I ran out the front entrance, and the car suddenly started up and peeled out an exit at the other end of the parking lot. It was too far away to get a license plate number. I marched back inside and up to the desk clerk.

"Can I help you?" he asked in a scratchy voice.

"Are we the only ones staying in the hotel?" I asked.

"Uh, yes, right now that's true."

"Has anyone been here since we left for dinner?"

"Why, no. Is there a problem?"

"Are the other entrances locked at night?"

"Yes, but not until ten p.m. Is there a problem?" he repeated.

I searched his face, but couldn't tell if he was lying.

"I think someone's been in our room," I said.

"I don't think so." He stared me in the eye. "I've been here all evening. Is anything missing?"

"I'm not sure."

"If there is, let me know and we can call the sheriff."

I held his gaze for a moment, then thanked him and went back to the room. I was locked out. I knocked softly on the door and called Willie's name. I saw a shadow in front of the peephole and then the door opened.

"Reed, what was that all about?" Willie asked. "I wasn't sure if I should follow you, or what. I finally decided to stay and look around."

"Was anything taken?"

She shook her head. "No."

I gestured at the window. "I think someone was watching us."

She glanced at the window, shuddered, and ran her hands up and down her arms. "This place *is* eerie."

I nodded. "I wanted you to stay here in case there was any trouble."

She put her hands on her hips. "I can take care of myself. My dad was a cop, remember? I know how to shoot a gun and protect myself. But when you go off half-cocked, sometimes I think I need to take care of *you*."

"Ouch."

"Besides," she gestured at my backpack, "you left your gun in there, so I had plenty of protection."

"Yeah, well..." I shrugged. "I wasn't planning on shooting anyone." The truth is, I don't like to carry the Glock. My thinking is much like TV detective Jim Rockford's: I don't want to carry a gun because I don't want to shoot anybody.

"Is everything okay?" she asked.

"Let's be careful," I said, "even though the desk clerk says we're alone here."

"Good." She slid out of her dress and lay down on the bed. "No one will hear us."

I smiled as I walked toward her.

» » » » »

Afterward, Willie snuggled close to me. "That was great."

"I couldn't agree more." Outside the window, a car passed by. She tensed slightly. "What?" I asked.

"I do want many more years of this," she said. "A long, happy life together."

"So do I."

She ran her hand across my chest. "You need to be more careful. What would've happened if you had gotten into a jam outside? That impulsiveness will get you into trouble."

"Yes, ma'am."

She pinched my arm.

"Ouch!"

"I'm serious," she said. "Promise me you won't take unnecessary risks."

I turned on my side to face her. "Where's this coming from?"

"When I was waiting for you to come back, I couldn't help but think what if something happened to you."

"Willie, we've talked about this before. I promise I'll be careful."

She smiled at me, and we lay together. When the air conditioner shut off, we could hear the occasional car drive by, and coyotes howling in the distance. Willie finally fell asleep, but I stayed awake for a long time. Every noise had me wondering if someone was trying to get into the room. If it were just me here, I'd have been less worried, but there was no way in hell I was going to let anything happen to Willie. I wanted a long, happy life together, too, just as she did.

At dawn, as soft light crept into the room, I dozed off.

# CHAPTER TWELVE

Hours later, I bolted awake. Sunlight was streaming through the open window. I sat up and looked around. The room was empty, but then I heard the shower running. I checked the time. Just after ten. I stretched, got up, and walked over to the window. The 4-Runner was sitting by itself in the parking lot. The water shut off and the bathroom door opened.

"You're up," Willie said. She had a towel wrapped around herself, and she was using one hand to comb her wet hair.

"How long have you been awake?" I asked.

"A couple hours. I knew you didn't sleep well, so I left you alone. I wanted to go for a run, but figured maybe I shouldn't, after last night –"

"Good thinking," I murmured.

"I went to the pool for a while," she continued. "And I tried to talk to that young desk clerk about Sagebrush and the mayor, but he wouldn't say anything."

I smiled at her. "Still in detective mode?"

"Just helping out."

"So no problems? No one watching us?"

She shook her head as she came over and kissed me. "Do you want to go soon?"

"Sure. I'll take a shower and we can go."

She nodded, then sat on the bed and checked her phone as I went into the bathroom. Half an hour later, we had checked out and we stopped for a late breakfast – or early lunch – at the same café. A different group of patrons was in attendance this morning, mostly farmers nursing cups of coffee and talking, and they were as slyly watchful of us as the crowd at dinner the previous night had been.

We ate a quiet meal without bothering to ask anyone questions, and we were soon on the road. By now, gray clouds had rolled in from the west, obscuring the sun. I was feeling sleepy, and I had Willie drive. I leaned back and dozed until my cell phone rang. I pulled it from my pocket.

"It's Cal," I said.

"Maybe he found out something about the trust."

"I hope so." I swiped the screen and answered.

"It was actually easier to find the Holder trust than I thought," Cal said, jumping right into the case.

"Really?"

"Yeah, because it's named the 'Holder Trust' and not something else. But I still had to dig around a while to find it. It looks like there was a lot of money put into the trust initially, but I don't know where those funds came from. It's been set up for over forty years. Each of the Holder kids – Jennifer, Marcia, and Toby – get a yearly stipend when they turn twenty-one, and Alvin Holder can sign off on a distribution of money at other times."

"Nice."

"You'd think, but the stipend isn't that much. The kids get the bulk of the money when Alvin and his wife die."

"What's the point of the trust? To mitigate tax liability?"

"That'd be my guess. Here's the kicker, though. It looks like the trust purchased a house in Denver in 1985, and has been paying bills for the place since that time."

I sat up straighter. "So the mortgage, utility bills, and things like that have been paid by the Holder Trust?"

"Yes."

"But nothing points to Marcia Holder owning the house."

"Correct."

"Is the trust paying for a mortgage or expenses for the other kids?"

"It paid for some land for both, but that's it, other than a small yearly stipend for each."

"Huh," I said. "Okay, text me the address."

"Will do."

"Thanks, I appreciate the help.

"No problem. Tell Willie 'hi' for me."

I ended the call and told Willie 'hi' as instructed.

"Good news?" she asked.

"I hope so." I related what Cal had said.

She sighed when I finished. "I hope this isn't a wild goose chase. Gina really wants to know what's going on."

"Yeah, but if she finds out her father kidnapped her, and kept her from her mother all these years…"

"That would be traumatic."

I nodded, then pointed to my phone and the address Cal had texted. "I'll drop you off at home, and then I'm going to see if Marcia Holder lives at that house, and try to talk to her."

"Sounds good."

We listened to music for the rest of the drive, and I watched for anyone following us. If there was someone tailing us, I never noticed. When we arrived in Denver, I left Willie at the condo and headed to the house paid for by the Holder Trust.

» » » » »

The address Cal had given me was on Emerson Street in the Alamo Placita neighborhood, a nice area of older homes a few miles southeast of downtown. The Holder house was a small, pale-green two-story with a large covered porch, and a huge maple tree in front. It was almost three when I found the house. I parked a few houses down the street and sat for a while in the car.

On the drive back from Sagebrush – when I wasn't dozing – I'd mulled over how to approach Marcia Holder, if I established that she lived in this house. Should I come right out and tell her about Gina Smith? Hearing news of her missing daughter after all these years could be exciting, but it could also be deeply upsetting. And given all the mystery surrounding the Holders, and Marcia, what if I didn't know the whole story? I'd finally decided to play it by ear and see what happened, but now that I was here, I was hesitating. This was not going to be an easy conversation.

I was still wavering when a woman in khaki shorts and a blue T-shirt came out the front door. She was slender, not very tall, with short brown hair and bangs covering a high forehead. From a distance, she looked a lot like the picture Annette had shown me. I also saw a resemblance to Gina Smith. She walked down the porch steps, glanced at the cloudy sky, then headed south, away from me.

Out for a walk while it was cool?

I didn't know, but I wasn't going to miss my opportunity. I hopped out of the 4-Runner, crossed the street, and hurried after her. She was walking fast as she crossed East Fourth Avenue. I waited for a car to drive by, then followed. Partway down the block was the entrance to Alamo Placita Park, which took up most of the block. The park had a playground and picnic area, but it was best known for its intricately designed floral displays. I'd brought Willie here a time or two, for a romantic walk after we'd gone to dinner. However, I didn't have time to mull too long on that, as the woman was crossing the grass in the park. She finally slowed down.

I drew closer and called out, "Marcia Holder?"

She turned around. "Yes?" She gazed at me, her expression part curiosity, part caution.

"I'm Reed Ferguson." Since I'd spooked Jennifer Madisen by telling her I was a private investigator, I decided not to share that information right now. "I'm looking into your baby's disappearance."

I watched her face, waiting for her reaction, thinking she'd be desperate for any news. *Why are you looking for her, and what do you know?* And most importantly, *has she been found?*

"Go away." With that, she whirled around and stepped up her pace.

*That* was not what I expected.

# CHAPTER THIRTEEN

"Ms. Holder?" I trotted after her.

"Leave me alone or I'll call the police," she hollered over her shoulder.

I stopped. "All right," I said, then reached in my pocket for my phone. "Let's call them and we can talk about the disappearance of Victoria in 1985."

She spun around and held up a hand. "Don't do that."

"Why?"

"Who are you?" She walked slowly toward me, alarm etched on her face. "And how do you know all this?"

Instead of answering, I studied her. "You look like her."

"Who?"

"Gina Smith." She paled, and then I added, "Or is it Victoria Holder?"

Now she was as white as a ghost. She stumbled over to the park entrance and sank down onto a flagstone step. I walked over and sat down next to her.

"Tell me –" She choked up, but then recovered herself. "Tell me what you know," she repeated firmly as she twisted the hem of her shorts in her hand.

The sky was dark, the air cool but humid, and I wiped sweat off my brow.

"I'm a private investigator," I said, then told her everything I'd learned since Gina Smith had hired me. She didn't say anything when I finished, but gazed around the park. At the other end, people were with their children at the playground, but no one was near us. I doubted she noticed the beautiful flower displays throughout the park.

She finally eyed me carefully. "My father didn't send you?"

I shook my head.

"No, of course he wouldn't," she mumbled. "I have things on him, too."

"What do you mean by that?"

She waved a hand dismissively. "Who sent you?"

*That was an odd thing to ask*, I thought but didn't say. "I was hired by Gina Smith," I repeated. "She wanted help finding her birth mother." I left out the part about her suspicions that her father had murdered her mother. "Why are you worried about your father?"

"What do you know about him?"

I shrugged. "Everyone in Sagebrush says he's done a great job managing the city."

"But?"

"I don't think they like him."

She let out a bitter laugh. "He can be personable, and charming, when he wants to be. But underneath he's a hard man."

I shifted position and looked at her directly. "If Gina is your kidnapped baby, why don't you want to know about her?"

She took a long time to answer. I waited. "I already do," she finally whispered.

I stared at her, stunned. "You've been keeping in touch?"

"With … John?" She shook her head. "Not directly. I've watched my daughter from afar." She thought for a while. I again waited. "I'm not sure how you tracked me down," she began, "but yes, I had a baby, back in '85. I met John – that's how you know him – when I was in high school. He worked at the dairy plant, but I saw him around town and at church. We talked, and I really liked him. We fell in love. It would've been a scandal if my father had found out because I was so young and John was much older. And Pastor Sheehan would've been irate as well. Then I got pregnant. I wanted to have the baby, and John agreed. Neither of us wanted to get rid of it or give it up for adoption. We really wanted to have the baby and raise it together." She sighed. "Obviously my family found out, that kind of thing can only be hidden for so long. My mother cried, and my father was furious. He was a very mean, controlling man, and he refused to let me see John after that, but John and I managed to sneak around behind his back." She frowned. "We talked about running away together, and then, about a month before I was due to have the baby, we did. I won't tell you where we went –"

"Russell, Kansas," I interrupted.

She gave me an appraising look. "Kudos to you. You've done your homework. Yes, we made it as far as Russell, Kansas, and I went into premature labor. We went to the hospital, and John just told them he was a friend of mine. I didn't know what to do when they asked me my name at the admissions desk. I knew I shouldn't use my real name. But by that time, labor was coming on pretty hard, and I was so scared, and I guess I just panicked. I gave them my sister's name: Jenny Madison."

I stopped her there. "Madison with an 'o'?"

"I guess that's how they spelled it."

"So," I went on, "even though you were trying to hide your identity, you gave them your *sister's* name? Seriously?" This sounded so crazy to me.

"I know, I know … I told you – I was 17 years old and in hard labor and the baby was coming early and I was running away from home." She turned a deep red. "It wasn't smart, I'll grant you that, but I adored my sister, and her name just popped into my head, so that's what I told them. John got mad at me for doing that, but at that point, I really didn't care. They filled out the paperwork, and that was it. I didn't have a driver's license or any ID with me, so they just thought I was a dumb teenager without insurance." She shrugged. "And after Victoria was born, someone came around to get information for the official birth certificate. I didn't name the baby's father, and I just told them 'Jenny Madison' as my name."

I held up a hand. "Wait – so your admissions information was under 'Jenny Madison', so the legal birth certificate lists that name, but the keepsake birth certificate that Gina found listed your name as 'Marsha Jenny Madison.'" I spelled out Marsha. "Where did *that* combination come from?"

She let out a tiny laugh. "Let's see … how *did* that happen? It's kind of hard to remember. I think by that time, the nurses had heard John calling me 'Marcia', which was a little weird since I'd given my name as Jenny. So I told one of the nurses that 'Marcia' was a nickname of mine. Turns out that she was the one who filled out the keepsake birth certificate for us, and she must have misunderstood my explanation, because she wrote in my 'nickname' as my first name on that certificate, that they gave me before we left the hospital. I guess she didn't even spell it right. I suppose on one of those keepsake things, it didn't matter so much." She got a faraway look in her eyes. "I remember her now. That nurse was nice. She had a big, bubbly personality. I think she may have suspected we were lying about a lot of stuff, but she didn't say anything."

"What happened after you had the baby?"

"Once I was released, we planned to go to the East Coast and vanish. But I needed a few days to rest, so we stayed in a hotel in Russell." She stared off into the distance, and her voice lowered. A car drove by behind us, and I leaned forward to hear her better. "I'd fallen asleep. The next thing I knew, there was shouting, and someone was fighting, but I don't remember it all. I found out later I'd fallen and banged my head on the nightstand. I was knocked out and had a concussion, and it affected my memory. I remember hearing my father's voice. He was screaming it had to stop. The next thing I remember, I was back home, in my room. A prisoner. My father was livid. He said John was gone, and that I was never to see him again. And he kept saying that he would put the baby up for adoption. I begged him not to, but before he could do anything, John came back without his knowing." She shook her head. "I still don't know how John sneaked around without anyone knowing. Anyway, we made a plan for John to take the baby and leave. He had everything worked out, like he always did. One night when everyone was asleep, he came by the house and took Victoria. I pretended that she'd been kidnapped, but I don't think my father believed me. He wanted to know where John was, and I told him John had gone back East. He beat me, but I refused to tell him anything. What really happened was John and I had decided that he'd go to Denver. He created a new identity for himself and for Victoria, got a job, and disappeared within the big city. I have no idea how he managed to do that. I've never had the opportunity to really sit down and talk with him about that time. It sounds almost impossible that he could cope with all that. But when he took the baby, he told me that no matter what, he'd take good care of her and that he'd do whatever he had to do to keep her safe and with him. And he has.

"Anyway, for a long time, I didn't know anything. Then John got in touch – we'd set up a way for him to leave a message near a big rock in a field west of town – and I knew that he was okay and in Denver. After that, I begged my father to let me move away. I told him I was devastated. There were too many memories in town, and everyone pitied me – that poor, sad girl. I couldn't stand it anymore. He finally relented, but he wanted the trust to pay for everything."

I crossed my arms. "Wait, why wouldn't your father just kick you out? There was no baby anymore, and you'd already … disgraced him."

"He still wanted to control me. And if he paid for things, he could keep tabs on me."

"Why would he need to do that?"

"Because I threatened to tell everyone that he sent people after me, and about him beating me. There was no way he wanted that to come out."

"That's *all* you have on him?"

"Well…" She hesitated, then nodded. I wasn't sure I believed her. Did she have something else on him, something she could blackmail him with?

"Truthfully, a part of me was okay with him paying," she said. "I was still young, from a small town. I'd been sheltered my whole life. The big city terrified me. All I wanted was to be able to watch Victoria from afar." She hung her head. "I let him pay. Maybe that's bad, but…"

I mulled that over, then said, "What did your mother or your siblings do about your father and how he was treating you?"

She laughed without mirth. "My mother was upset about the pregnancy, but I think more because of what my father might do to her, for letting it happen – like she could've stopped us. I don't know what Toby and Jennifer thought, but they didn't do anything. They were as scared of my father as anyone else." She let out another wry laugh. "It's funny. Toby's the spitting image of my father, looks and sounds like him, but he's not mean like my father. I don't know why he didn't do anything, except that he had his own problems with drugs, so I don't know how much he was paying attention to what was happening to me."

"I notice you never say 'Dad.'"

"He wasn't one, not really."

I let that sink in. "So you moved to Denver, and…"

"John and I devised a way that I could see him with her," she said. "They kept to a schedule, and I knew where they'd be on most days. Even so, I hardly saw them, because I was worried that my father had people watching me. But it was something, a way to keep connected with my daughter. I was careful about it, just in case." She bit her lip. "My father might've been spying on me, at the beginning, but I think it stopped since he knew what I could do to him." She gazed at me. "I live a very quiet life here. The trust pays all my bills, and I don't do anything to draw attention to myself. And when my father dies, he can't control the money anymore."

"You're sure about that?"

She nodded. "Once he dies, the trust dissolves and I inherit a third of the money."

"Where did all the money come from?"

"The dairy plant, I guess. Although I don't know how the plant makes that much, for him to have as much money as he has." She shrugged. "But what do I know about business?"

I put everything she said together. It was quite a story. Certainly not what I expected. I wondered what Gina would think of all this.

"So this whole scheme with John was because of your father?" I asked.

"Yes."

"And you never talk to John?"

"No. We can't risk that."

"Do you still love him?"

"Yes," she whispered.

Thunder rumbled and we looked up.

She stood up. "It looks like it might start raining. I should go home."

I got up as well. "I'm left with one question: Do you want to meet with your daughter?"

"Very much so." She could barely get the words out. "But you can't let my father know."

"Why? After all this time, does it matter what he thinks?"

"You *can't* let anyone know! Just her."

I held up my hands in supplication. "Okay. We can arrange that."

We started walking back up Emerson.

"But I want you there," she said.

"Why?"

"In case anything goes wrong."

"What could go wrong?"

"You've been poking around Sagebrush. What if someone

followed you?"

"No one did." Although I couldn't be certain. Had someone followed Willie and me home? I'd watched, but had I missed a tail? However, I was sure someone had broken into our hotel room, and someone may have been watching us in Sagebrush. "I'll do whatever you want," I said. I didn't know why her father, or anyone else in Sagebrush, would care if she met her daughter after all these years, but if she was scared about it, then that's all that mattered. I smiled to calm her.

"Thank you."

A flash of lightning split the dark sky and she quickened her pace. I did as well.

"I'll get in touch with Gina," I said. "When do you want to meet?"

"Anytime. I'll make it work."

We walked the rest of the way in silence.

"What's your phone number?" I asked as we paused in front of her house.

She told me and I put it in my phone.

"Thank you," she said, then added, "Be careful."

"I will," I replied, although I didn't see why I needed to be.

She started to say something, then choked up. Without a word, she turned and ran up the front porch. I waited until she'd disappeared into the house. A few big raindrops pelted me, but no real rain came as I rushed back to my car. I got in, thinking that this case was nearly finished and that it was one of the easiest I'd had in a while.

Why do I keep letting myself fall for those thoughts?

# CHAPTER FOURTEEN

As I sat in the 4-Runner and called Gina Smith, the rain stopped. She answered after the second ring.

"Any news?" she asked.

"Are you sitting down?"

"What? Tell me."

"I found your mother."

"Oh, I –" She choked up, just like her mother had earlier. "I can't believe it." She sniffled. "Hold on."

I heard a clunk, as if she'd put the phone down. I gave her as much time as she needed. She gathered herself, got back on the phone and said she was okay, and then I told her about meeting Marcia Holder.

"I can't believe it," she repeated. "You actually found her."

I glanced at Marcia's house. "She'd like to meet you."

"Where? When?"

"Wherever and whenever it works for you."

"How about tonight? I've waited so long for this, I don't think I could wait a second longer. Dad picked up Ethan earlier to take him to a movie, so I have the night free."

I glanced at the clock on the dashboard. It wasn't even five o'clock yet. "Could you be at the Starbucks on the Mall by six?"

"Yes."

"Let me call Marcia and see what she says."

I called Marcia, thinking that if she didn't answer, I'd go back to the house and talk to her in person. But she picked up, and agreed to meet Gina and me at the Starbucks. I called Gina back, and she answered right away.

"I'm already on the road."

"Good," I said. "Marcia will be there by six. One thing, though."

"What?"

"You're sure your dad's not following you?" I glanced around to make sure no one was following *me*.

"Positive. He's at the movies right now."

"Okay. Marcia's paranoid about anyone finding out about this."

"No one will," she said. "Tell you what. I'll meet with her inside the Starbucks. That way, no one will even see us unless they come inside."

"Or they look in the window."

"You're paranoid, too."

"Part of the job," I said. "I'll sit outside, just in case your father decides to show up again."

"He's at the movies," she said again with emphasis.

"Right. If he shows up, I'll stall him before he can get inside. There's a back way out of that Starbucks, past the bathrooms at the back of the building. You and Marcia go out that way."

"Is all this necessary?"

"Probably not, but Marcia's nervous."

"I'm nervous, too, but in a good way," she said. "This is so ama-zing! After all this time, I'm going to meet my birth mother. Thank you,

Reed."

"No problem."

I let her chatter for a bit, ended the call, then headed for the Six-teenth Street Mall. I had to park a few blocks away in a metered spot, and then walk to the Starbucks. I waited outside, and Marcia showed up a few minutes later. We went inside and bought macchiatos, and then waited near the counter where I could see through the window onto the mall, but far back enough that it would be difficult for someone outside to see us.

"I'm so nervous," Marcia said breathlessly.

I nodded. "So is Gina."

"I'm sure."

She barely sipped her drink, and kept flicking her hair as she looked around. I watched people hurrying up and down the mall, and finally, a few minutes before six, Gina materialized from the crowd. Her pace was quick as she crossed the outside patio and entered the store. She immediately saw us, but suddenly her legs seemed to be leaden, and she walked slowly over. Tension filled the air as the two women sur-veyed each other.

"Hi," Marcia said, a warble in her voice.

"It's really you," Gina murmured.

They embraced awkwardly, and then glanced at me.

"I'll go outside so you can talk in private," I said.

They barely acknowledged me as they moved to a table near the back. I moseyed outside and sat at a table. The dark clouds overhead hadn't opened up yet, but the air still felt like rain was coming. The mall was busy and I watched people, keeping an eye out for John Smith, or anyone else who looked suspicious. Time ticked slowly by. Then I noticed a man in jeans and a black T-shirt loitering across the street. Was he looking my way? I watched him for a while. He seemed to make eye contact with me, and then he moved off.

"Huh," I said to myself. *Was* I being paranoid?

At eight, the Starbucks closed, and Gina walked out the door. I stood up and looked past her.

"Where's Marcia?"

She jerked a thumb toward the Starbucks. "She went out the back way."

"How did it go?"

She smiled. "Good." Then she shrugged. "A little uncomfortable. She told me what happened all those years ago. I almost don't believe it. And I find myself so angry with Alvin Holder."

"Uh-huh."

"And we talked about Ethan, and my career, things like that. We have a lot of catching up to do."

"I'm sure."

She reached out a hand. "Thank you, for everything. Will you send me a bill? And I'll take care of it right away."

"Absolutely."

"Willie said you're a great detective. I believe it."

I felt my face getting warm. "Thank you."

I walked halfway down the street with her, and then we parted ways. The storm was again threatening, and wind whipped at me as I hurried to my car. It started to sprinkle, and by the time I arrived home, it was pouring. Since Willie uses the garage behind our building, I had to park on the street, and I was soaked before I got up to our building. As I crossed the front porch to go to the stairs on the side of the building, my downstairs neighbors Ace and Deuce Smith came out of their condo, both with umbrellas in their hands.

"Hey, Reed," Ace said.

"Hi, Reed." Deuce waved a hand at me.

Ace and Deuce are my friends and sometimes assistants. They look almost the same, with blond hair and eyes as gray as a snowy sky. Neither is necessarily the sharpest tool in the shed. But what they lack in smarts, they make up for in enthusiasm. They're loyal and fun, and Willie and I love them.

"You want an umbrella?" Ace held his out.

"It's a little late for that," I said.

"We have ours." Deuce wiggled his compact umbrella at me. "So we don't get wet."

"Good thinking," I muttered.

"Are you on a case?" Ace asked.

"Just finished," I said as I wiped rain off my face.

Disappointment filled Deuce's face. "Bummer." He glanced toward my ankle, looking for my gun and holster. "Did you have to shoot anyone?" It was his dream to work with me and get in a shootout. Somehow my Jim Rockford philosophy hadn't rubbed off on him.

"No, this was an easy case," I said.

"Okay," they said in unison.

"We're going to B 52s," Ace said. "You want to come?"

B 52s, a pool hall near our condos, is our favorite hangout.

"Yeah," I said. "Willie and I might come over in a bit."

"Oh, Willie's home?" Deuce asked. Both brothers loved Willie, and she was sweet with them.

I nodded toward the stairs. "She's waiting for me."

"Oh, okay." Ace nudged Deuce. "Let's go. They'll come if they can."

Deuce waved at me. "See you."

With that, they both opened their umbrellas and hurried around to the back of the building. I took the steps three-at-a-time upstairs. When I walked inside, Willie was at the kitchen table with her laptop in front of her. She glanced up at me and smothered a laugh.

"Have you heard of an umbrella?" she asked.

I rolled my eyes at her. "I left it here."

She chuckled. "Good place for it. How'd it go?"

"We've been invited to B 52s with Ace and Deuce. How about I change clothes and I'll tell you all about my afternoon?"

"That sounds like fun."

And that's how I thought my case had ended. Until I received a call from Gina three days later.

"Reed!"

"Gina?" I didn't like the dread in her voice. "How are things with you and –"

That's as far as I got before she blurted out, "She's gone."

# CHAPTER FIFTEEN

"What do you mean she's gone?" I asked.

"Well, I don't know that she's *gone*, but she hasn't returned my calls."

"Okay, let's back up," I said. "When was the last time you talked to Marcia?"

"Friday night, at the Starbucks. She and I agreed that we'd talk the next day, and I called her and left a message, but she never called back. I've left a few more messages, even asking her to just text me if she doesn't want to talk anymore, that I'd understand, but I haven't heard a word from her. Have you?"

"No, but why would I?"

"I don't know. I thought maybe if she was upset after talking to me, she might tell you about it."

"She didn't," I said.

"I don't even know where she lives. This is horrible." I could hear the tears about to come. "I can't have just found my mother and then have her disappear!"

"Don't jump to conclusions. I'll try calling her, and if she doesn't answer, I'll go over to her house and see if she's there."

"Can I come, too?"

I wavered. "If for some reason she doesn't want to see you, that's probably not a good idea."

"Yeah, you're right." She was disappointed. "Call me the minute you know something, okay?"

"I will."

I got off the phone with her and tried Marcia, but she didn't answer. I left a message explaining that I was concerned about her, and would she please call me back as soon as she could. Then I waited to see if she was screening her calls. But after ten minutes with no response, I grabbed my Glock and my keys, left a note for Willie, who was at work, and ran out the door.

» » » » »

Fifteen minutes later, I parked in front of Marcia's house. It was about 1:30, and the street was quiet. I sat and studied the house for a minute. Cream-colored curtains in the front windows were drawn, but nothing seemed out of the ordinary. I let a car drive by, got out and ambled up the porch steps. I rang the bell and waited, then knocked on the door. No answer. I banged a little harder. Nothing. I glanced around, assured myself no one was watching me, then grabbed the doorknob and twisted. It didn't budge.

I tried calling Marcia again, but it went directly to voice mail. I didn't bother leaving a message. I looked up and down the street. Still quiet. I made a quick decision, and stepped off the porch and hurried around the side of the house through a chain-link gate into the back. The yard was postage stamp-sized, with flower beds along one side and a tiny garden in the corner. At the end was a detached garage. I walked over and looked in a side window. No car was inside, and I didn't see Marcia.

I tapped on the window and called out, just to be sure, then went to the back door of the house, knocked, and tried the knob. Locked. I peered through a window into a small kitchen. It appeared neat and clean. And empty. I returned to the front porch, not sure what to do.

Were Gina and I overreacting? What if Marcia just wasn't here or had gone out of town? Or what if her father somehow found out about her meeting with Gina? Why would he possibly care after all these years? I thought about my options. I could watch the house for a day or two to see if she returned. Boring, yes, but I'd know whether she was still in town. I could call the police to do a welfare check, but if she wasn't home when they dropped by, that would end that. They wouldn't break in without a good reason to believe something was wrong. And I didn't have that reason.

I, on the other hand, could let myself in, just to make sure that nothing sinister had happened. In the last few years as a PI, I'd become adept at picking locks. I noticed a welcome mat in front of the door and checked under it. No key. I was debating whether to pick the lock or not when an older woman in blue capris and a sleeveless blouse emerged from the house next door. Her gold jewelry glinted in the sun and contrasted oddly with her pink tennis shoes. Her gray hair didn't move with the breeze as she walked down the sidewalk. Hm. This woman could be my mother's fashion-twin.

"Excuse me," I called out to her.

She turned, shielded her eyes, and then saw me. "Yes?"

I started down the porch steps. "Do you know if Marcia is a-round?"

She started across the lawn. "I haven't talked to her in a few days."

"Have you seen her at all since Friday night?"

"I just told you I haven't seen her."

"Well, no, you said you hadn't talked to her." I held up a hand. "Just clarifying."

She put her hands on her hips, and her pink lips pressed into a miffed line that also reminded me of my mother. Yikes. My mother, by the way, does "miffed" really well. But this woman was pretty good at it, too. She stared at me. "Who are you?"

I took out a business card and handed it to her.

"Reed Ferguson. A private investigator? Is Marcia in some kind of trouble?"

I shrugged. "I'm not sure. My client was supposed to talk to Marcia a few days ago, and she's left messages, but Marcia hasn't called her back."

"Maybe Marcia doesn't want to talk to her," she said bluntly.

"That's a possibility. I was wondering if I should ask the police to do a welfare check. Or is there a way to get into the house to make sure she's not inside and can't get to the phone?"

She studied me. "What if she's out of town?" Then she wrinkled her brow. "Although she usually asks me to water her houseplants and get her mail if she goes anywhere."

"Does she travel much, Miss…"

"Doris," she said. "And no, she doesn't, just to the mountains, sometimes."

"You know her pretty well?"

"I wouldn't say well. Marcia doesn't talk much about herself, but she's nice. We talk gardening, and TV shows. She's invited me over for coffee once in a while."

"Has she ever talked about her family?"

She shook her head. "Not that I recall."

"Did you see Marcia on Friday night?"

She pursed her lips and thought. "Now that you mention it, I heard her come through the back. I was working in the back yard. But I haven't seen or heard her since."

"Have you seen anyone hanging around here, maybe watching her house?"

She wrapped her arms around herself. "I did see a guy the other day. He was parked in a dark car down the street for a while. I'm getting concerned about all your questions. Is that man after Marcia?"

"I have no idea, but if you see him again, I'd call the police. It's probably nothing, but better safe than sorry."

She trembled.

"Have you ever seen a man around here with darker gray hair, kind of a square jaw? About average height?" I did my best to describe John Smith.

"No, he doesn't sound familiar." She harrumphed and looked past me at Marcia's house. "Now you're scaring me," Doris snapped. "I think we should go inside and check. There's no harm in that. I've got a key. Let me get it and I'll go in with you." The underlying tone implied, "I've got my eye on you."

I suppressed a smile and waited while she went to her house. She returned a minute later, waving a key at me.

"Now we'll see if there's a problem," she announced. She moved past me and up to the door, then opened it and called out, "Yoo-hoo, Marcia? Are you in there?"

Silence.

"Marcia?" Doris walked inside and then said, "Oh my, what's this?"

I followed her into an open foyer. To the right was a living and dining area, and beyond that a kitchen. Down the hall was a staircase leading up to the second floor. A small table to our left was toppled over, and a broken faux-Tiffany lamp lay on the floor.

"What's that?" She gestured at some dark drops on the hardwood floor.

I bent down and studied it. "I think it's blood."

She reached down to pick up the lamp, then stopped. "Oh, I probably shouldn't touch it, in case this is a crime scene."

I moved over toward the lamp and examined it without touching it. "I can't tell if there's any blood on it."

"Why would there be blood on it?"

I stood up straight. "If Marcia hit someone with it. Or they hit her."

A hand flew to her chest. "Oh my gosh." Then she whirled around. "Marcia?"

She started through the house, with me on her heels. We checked the kitchen, a small home office, and spare bedroom on the main floor, a master suite upstairs, and an unfinished basement, but Marcia was not there. We ended back in the foyer.

"Other than that mess," she gestured at the broken lamp, "this place looks like it always does. Do you think something happened to Marcia?"

"I doubt it," I said, more to comfort her than because I believed it.

The truth was, a broken lamp and what might be drops of blood on the floor did not constitute a potential crime. There could be a perfectly rational explanation for it. In my gut, though, I knew differently. However, knowing it and proving it were two different things.

"We should call the police," Doris said.

I nodded. She pulled out an ancient flip phone and dialed 911, and explained the situation. I wanted to check around the house more thoroughly, but Doris had her eyes on me.

When she got off the phone, I asked, "Did Marcia ever mention a daughter?"

"She didn't have kids," she said. "I don't think she ever even married."

Then she went to the door, and we waited in awkward silence for a few minutes until a police cruiser drove up and parked behind my 4-Runner. A burly officer with a pencil-thin mustache got out and marched up the steps.

He eyed me and tipped his head at Doris. "Ma'am." His nameplate read, "Swanson."

Doris launched into why she'd called him. He listened politely, and every once in a while he looked at me.

"And you are?" he asked me when she finished.

I told him, and explained about how Gina had been trying to reach Marcia since Saturday.

"So you've got suspicions that something might've happened to Miss Holder, but that's all."

I nodded. His radio squawked and he lowered the volume. He knelt down and checked the drops on the floor. "Yeah, I'd say it's blood." He looked at the lamp, his face impassive. Then he stood up. "And nothing else in the house has been disturbed?"

"Not that we can tell," Doris said.

He scratched his head. "There's no real proof that a crime has been committed. Ms. Holder could've broken the lamp by accident and cut herself on a piece of glass."

Doris waved a hand at the broken lamp. "Why not clean it up?"

Swanson shrugged. "Maybe she got called away, and she'll get to it when she returns." He frowned. "I can file a missing persons report, and someone will check the hospitals. Keep an eye out for any strange activity around the neighborhood, and report anything to us." He averted his eyes from Doris's glare. "Look, I wish there was more I could do..." His voice trailed off.

Doris had her hands on her hips again. "Well." She was peeved he wasn't doing more.

Swanson thanked us and made his escape before Doris could voice her displeasure.

"That was useless," she grumbled as he drove off. "What if something's happened to Marcia?"

"I'll see what I can find out," I said. "You have my card. If you see any strangers around here, or if Marcia shows up, let the police know, but give me a call, too."

She nodded. "I will."

"Are you around a lot?"

"Some."

I thought for a second. "I might have my two buddies watch the house for a few days, just so we don't miss Marcia if she shows up." I described Ace and Deuce, and their cars.

"Okay, good to know." She bit her lip. "I don't know Marcia that well, but I still hope nothing's happened to her."

I agreed with her sentiment.

# CHAPTER SIXTEEN

On the way home, I called Gina Smith.

"Did you find her?" she asked.

"No." I told her what I knew, ending with, "The broken lamp could be something innocent, just like the cop told me."

"Do you really believe that, or do you think someone hurt Marcia?"

My mind raced over everything I knew, including all the strange behavior I'd encountered in Sagebrush. "I have my suspicions."

"Why would anyone care whether I met my birth mother?" Her voice was almost a wail.

"That's the question of the day."

"I want you to find her," she said without hesitation. "I'll pay whatever it takes."

"All right. At this point, I need to talk to your dad. I know you don't want me to, but –"

"This changes everything," she said with conviction, and with a new confidence I hadn't heard in her before. "I'll call him and tell him what's going on, and arrange for you to meet him."

"Are you sure you want to do that?"

"I am now," she said. "I want to know what's going on."

"That's good, and the sooner the better."

"Oh, I won't let him put you off." A decidedly firm tone was in her voice. "I'll call you back."

I ended the call. Ten minutes later, I was knocking on the Goofballs' front door.

Ace answered in an old T-shirt and shorts, his hair messed up, his eyes tired. "Hey, Reed."

"No work today?" I asked. Ace works in the electronics department at Best Buy, and his hours vary. I never know what his schedule is.

"No, I'm off for a couple of days." He yawned. "I stayed up late playing video games."

"Want to help me?"

He was suddenly alert. "You on a new case?"

I shook my head. "The same one, as it turns out."

"What do you need?"

Now came the delicate part. Ace and Deuce loved to help me, but if it involved something boring, like a stakeout, not so much. So I had to make the boring sound thrilling, which wasn't easy.

"I need you to watch a house for me. A woman named Marcia Holder lives there."

"Oh, that sounds boring."

*See what I mean?*

"It's not," I said. I lowered my voice conspiratorially. "It actually could be quite dangerous." I was playing it up, and it worked.

"Oh?" Now he was all ears.

I nodded and described Marcia in detail. "If you see her, or notice any activity in the house, like lights on or noises coming from the house, call me. You can park across the street, where you can see through the chain-link fence into the back yard, and where the garage is. And if you see anyone else trying to get into the house, or watching the house, you let me know."

"Who else would get into the house?"

"I don't know. Possibly someone in a dark sedan. That's the dangerous part."

"Ah," he said, then hesitated. "Um, what if I have to go to the bathroom?"

I shrugged. "You can leave for that, just make it quick."

"Okay, I can do that."

I gave him the address and directions, then described the house. He grabbed pen and paper and wrote it all down.

"See if Deuce can help," I suggested. "Maybe he can spell you at night."

"Spell 'night' for me?"

I resisted a smile. "He can give you a break. Or stay with you, and you can keep each other company."

"Ah, I see." He grinned. "You can count on us."

"I know, thanks."

And now, between Marcia's next-door neighbor Doris and the Goofballs, if Marcia came home, someone should see her. My phone rang and I glanced at it. It was Gina.

"I've got to get this," I said.

"I'll change clothes and be on my way." He saluted me and closed the door.

I chuckled as I answered.

"I confronted Dad." Gina sucked in a breath. "I told him I'd tracked Marcia down, and that I wondered what he was hiding. He was *not* happy with me, and said I never should've tried to find her. But he's worried about Marcia, so he says he'll talk to you, even though he doesn't think he knows anything that will help."

"When?"

"Now, at his house."

"What's the address?"

She gave it to me. "It may be a waste of your time."

"We'll see."

» » » » »

John Smith lived in a quaint ranch house on Fillmore Street, near the University of Denver campus. The neighborhood was filled with small houses on big lots, or McMansions that had been built where tiny houses used to be. I parked and had barely walked up to the minuscule front porch when the door opened.

"Come on in," Smith said to me.

He showed me into a small living room furnished with a sage green couch and overstuffed chair that flanked a yellow brick fireplace. The carpet and walls were off-white, and the only decoration in the room was a painting of aspen trees that hung over the fireplace.

"Have a seat," he ordered.

I sat down on the couch and he took the chair. He was in gray slacks and a white shirt with the sleeves rolled up, his one nod to casual. He sat ramrod straight and stared at me with cold brown eyes.

"Gina should've never started down this path," he said with a headshake. Then he changed direction. "Are you sure Marcia didn't just leave for a few days? Maybe seeing her daughter overwhelmed her, and she needed some time to think."

"It's possible, but what if something did happen to her? Time is of the essence then."

"This is crazy," he muttered.

When he didn't offer anything more, I said, "I got Marcia's version of what happened back in 1985. How about telling me yours?"

"There's not much to say." He glanced away wistfully. "I was wandering a bit after college, working a series of odd jobs for years, not ready to settle down. I ended up in Sagebrush."

"Where'd you go to college?"

"Back east."

"Is that where you're from?"

"Yes." He arched an eyebrow slyly. "That's all you need to know."

"You were running away from something," I said.

He ignored that. "It doesn't matter now."

"What's your real name?"

He shook his head slowly. "You don't need to know that."

"What're you hiding?"

"My past doesn't have anything to do with this," he snapped.

"How do you know?"

He ignored that, took in a deep breath and let it out slowly. "When I got to Sagebrush, I started working at the dairy plant. I met Marcia and we fell in love, but since she was so much younger than I was, we kept it a secret. I'm sure she told you how her father could be."

I nodded.

"Then she got pregnant and we decided to leave town, away from all of it."

"All of what?"

He thought about his answer. "Her father. We left a month before she was due, and had gotten as far as Kansas when she had the baby." He stopped, and pain flashed in his eyes.

"What happened that night?"

"We were at the hotel and they suddenly showed up."

"Who?"

He again took time in answering, as if trying to decide how much to tell me. "They came for us, and there was a fight. Marcia tried to intervene, and she fell against the nightstand." He looked away. "She was out cold. I bent over to try to help her, and they knocked me down and tied me up. They left, carrying Marcia and the baby.

"I struggled for a while, but it didn't take me long to loosen the sloppy knots they'd tied. I got out of the room as fast as I could, but stayed to watch the hotel. They came back a while later – I think to kill me – and I saw that Marcia was in their car. I knew I couldn't rescue her right then." He put his head down for a moment. "I didn't know what to do. They left, and I assumed they took Marcia back to Sagebrush. I didn't know what Mayor Holder would do to her or the baby, so I sneaked back to Sagebrush and got in touch with Marcia."

"How did you avoid Holder in a small town like Sagebrush?"

He hesitated. "I was careful, I guess. He didn't know I was there, and that's all that mattered. Marcia and I worked out a plan that I'd come to Denver with the baby, and she'd try to move here at some point, if she could arrange something with her father. She just wanted to be close to Gina, but she was scared of what her father would do if he ever found out that she knew where Gina was. Once we decided that, I sneaked out to her house one night. She'd gotten the baby all ready to go, so I took the baby, and left." He stared at me. "I think you know the rest."

"Would Mayor Holder come after you, if he knew you'd taken

Gina?"

His jaw tightened. "Holder could be a tyrant. He had that town fooled."

I took that as a yes. "Have you had contact with Marcia over the years?"

He shook his head. "We couldn't risk it."

"You think Mayor Holder is so vengeful that he'd do something even years later?"

He didn't say anything to that.

"And you haven't talked to Marcia since she met Gina the other night?" I asked.

"No."

I gazed at him for a moment, sure that he was lying to me. Did Marcia's disappearance have something to do with his past? Had he talked to Marcia recently? If so, why not tell me?

"Would anyone else besides Mayor Holder be after Marcia?"

His eyes darted away from me and then back. "Like who?"

"Someone from your past."

"No," he said quickly.

"Someone in Sagebrush? Was someone besides Mayor Holder angry with the two of you?"

He shook his head. "It's nothing like that."

"Would Marcia just disappear and not come back?"

"I don't know." He blinked hard. "I hope nothing's happened to her."

"It would help if you told me everything."

"I have," he snapped. He recovered quickly. "What're you going to do next?"

I shrugged. "I'm going up to Sagebrush to talk to Mayor Holder."

"I doubt you'll get anywhere."

"I have to try."

"Be careful. He's slick."

"Thanks for the warning."

"You should leave the past in the past."

"I just want to find Marcia."

He frowned, then stood up and showed me to the door. As I walked down the sidewalk to my car, I frowned. Smith obviously cared about Marcia, even after all these years, but he was also not telling me everything. Why?

# CHAPTER SEVENTEEN

On the way home, I called Cal.

"What's up, O Great Detective?" he asked.

"You busy?"

"Not too much for you."

"Did you find anything on John Smith?"

"Not so far, sorry."

"I finally got his address. With that, you could track him down, right?"

"Of course. Have you been holding out on me?"

I laughed. "No, I just met him." I brought Cal up to speed on my investigation and my conversation with John Smith. "I don't trust the guy. I want a thorough background check on him. Dig deep, okay? And can you monitor his phone calls?"

"Sure. I'll call you when I get something."

"Thanks."

Willie was at work, so I left her a message telling her about Gina's call, that I was headed back to Sagebrush, and to call me when she could. I told her that I loved her, and not to worry. Then I turned on the music, but I wasn't really hearing it. I kept thinking about Marcia Holder, and hoping that nothing bad had happened to her. When I arrived home,

Deuce was coming out of his place.

"Hey, Reed, I'm going over to spell Ace." He emphasized "spell", as if he and I were in on a secret.

I winked at him. "Good thinking. I'll touch base with Ace in a little bit."

"He hasn't seen anything," he said, trying to be helpful.

"Okay." I patted him on the shoulder. "Thanks for your help. I hope it's not too boring."

"It'll be all right," he said, not convinced. "How long do you want me to stay?"

"Maybe ten o'clock or so?"

I could see him doing some calculations in his head, figuring out how long he would have to be bored.

"That won't be too bad," he said. "I was worried you'd want me to stay all night."

I shook my head. "No need for that, especially since you have to work tomorrow."

"Right. I'll do a good job watching the house. We'll call tonight if we see anything." He waved and left.

I hurried upstairs, packed some things in a duffel bag, and put my laptop in my backpack. Then I strapped on my Glock and ankle holster, and headed out. I stopped at a Subway for a quick bite and was on Interstate 70 by 4:30. At that time of day, traffic was at a crawl, but the farther I got from Denver, the lighter the traffic became. I put the 4-Runner on cruise control and enjoyed an uneventful drive across the eastern plains. The only thing that would've made the drive better would have been Willie sitting in the passenger seat.

Almost two hours later I turned north off the Interstate, and soon drove into Sagebrush. I stopped and got the same room at the Sagebrush Inn. I left my duffel bag on the bed, but kept my backpack with me. Then I drove to Annette Gessler's house. I parked, then strode up to the front door and knocked. She answered a moment later and her face went pale.

"What're you doing here?" she hissed.

"I found Marcia, but –"

She stepped out onto the porch and pulled the door shut behind her. "My husband's home, and I don't want him to hear us."

"Marcia's disappeared, and I'm worried someone may have hurt her."

A hand flew to her throat. "Oh no. What happened?"

I shrugged. "I don't know. She met her daughter, and then vanished. I can't share all the details now, but have you heard from Marcia?"

She glanced behind her, then said, "No, not a thing."

I scrutinized her carefully. "That's the truth?"

"Yes."

I believed her.

"You think Marcia may have come here?" she asked.

My mind flashed to the blood on the floor of Marcia's house. "Or she was brought here against her will."

She shivered. "They wouldn't do that."

"You mean the Holders?"

Her lips formed a thin line, and she nodded.

"Do you ever talk to the Holders?" I asked.

"Just when I see them around town, or at church. But nothing is said about Marcia or the baby. That's taboo."

"You don't socialize with them at all?"

"No! I don't know anything." She let out a big sigh. "I wish I did.

If you want to take on the Holders, go right ahead."

"I'm going to talk to Jennifer Madisen next." *If she doesn't slam the door in my face*, I thought, but didn't say.

"Well, you'll have a good shot tonight. It's poker night at the Lodge, so the sheriff will be there. But you're crazy to try. She won't talk to you."

"Does she go out with friends when he's playing poker?"

She shrugged. "Maybe, but she's more likely to spend the time with her horses."

"What do you know about Jennifer?"

"Not much."

"Did Marcia and Jennifer get along?"

"As far as I know. Jennifer's five years older than Marcia, and Marcia looked up to her sister."

"Did Jennifer ever leave town, to go to college or work after high school?"

"I don't think the mayor would've allowed her to leave town, for college or anything else. She worked at the dairy plant for a while, but she'd been dating Ben since high school, and they got married a couple of years after they graduated. She loved horses, so they bought ranch land and built a big house, and bought horses. They have two boys who both work out at the dairy plant. That was kind of her life, raising the kids, and the horses. She travels now, but never back then."

"What's Toby like?"

"He's good-looking, like his dad, but not mean, although Toby was wild for a while. That boy could drink, and I heard he was into drugs for a bit, too. But he straightened himself out, and he's done really well for himself with that farm equipment store."

"Why didn't he work at the plant?"

"He did, in high school and for a year or so after that, but I don't think the mayor was ready to give up control, and Toby was having his own troubles."

"With the drinking and drugging?"

She nodded. "And he was with a bad crowd, too. But then his friend Jay was murdered, and that seemed to change things for Toby."

My ears perked up. "When was his friend murdered?"

"1985."

"The same time that Marcia got pregnant, and her baby was kidnapped."

She frowned. "Jay's death didn't have anything to do with Marcia. He was hanging with a rough crowd, and there were rumors he was selling drugs."

"Did Jay grow up in Sagebrush?"

"No, his family moved here from Nebraska when he was in high school, and that's when he and Toby became friends. They worked together at the dairy plant, and hung out. Jay moved to Denver for a year or so, and came back married."

"How'd he die?"

"It was awful. He was shot in the back of the head. A farmer found his body out in a field south of town. They never found who did it. People wondered if it was some kind of a drug deal gone bad, but I don't know."

"Do you think Mayor Holder had anything to do with Jay's murder?"

"Good Lord, why would you jump to that conclusion?" she said harshly.

"It seems that the mayor comes up a lot around this town, and never in a good context."

"Well, I heard a few people say they thought he knew something, but that's it."

"What was Jay's last name?"

"Hmm, I don't remember. It's been so long ago…"

I thought for a second. "So after Jay died, Toby started his own business."

"Yes. I think he got good and scared about the direction of his own life."

"Did the mayor give him some start-up cash?"

She shrugged. "I have no idea. All I know is Toby opened the store when he was about twenty-two or so, and he's made a boatload of cash."

"There's that much money to be made in farm equipment?"

"I guess." She crossed her arms. "It was nice to see Toby do well." Then she glanced back at the door. "I should go."

"What does your husband do at Toby's store?" I asked quickly.

"He's Toby's second-in-command. He works with suppliers, and in sales, the front counter. He's been there for years."

I nodded. "If you hear from Marcia, or think of anything else, call me." I took out a card and started to hand it to her, but she pushed my hand away.

"I can't take that. What if my husband finds it? What'll I say to him?"

"Does it matter?"

She grimaced. "You don't know this town. Or the Holders."

"Fine. I'm staying at the Sagebrush Inn. Leave a message there."

"I will." She reached behind her and grabbed the doorknob. "I need to go."

Without another word, she spun around and let herself back into the house. I walked back to my car, and as I got in, I glanced at the house. A heavyset man with blond hair and a handlebar mustache was peering out the window at me. He had a frown on his face. Annette's husband? I found myself hoping I hadn't gotten her into trouble with him.

## CHAPTER EIGHTEEN

If I wanted to talk to Jennifer Madisen, it looked as if I'd have to take a chance and go to her house again. Not that I relished that idea, since she'd slammed the door in my face the last time and called her sheriff husband to run me off their property. The only good thing was that this time, her husband was supposed to be gone. If so, maybe she wouldn't want to bother him, and I could get her talking. It was a chance I'd have to take.

I admired a beautiful sunset as I drove away from the Gessler house. It took a few minutes to drive through town, and then I was on the highway. When I reached County Road 15, I noticed the heat of the day was dissipating, and I rolled down my window. Alfalfa had recently been harvested, and a pungent, earthy odor filled the 4-Runner. I soon approached the Madisen ranch. I turned down the dirt road and drove slowly around the circular drive. When I drew parallel with the house, I stopped. The house looked quiet in the approaching dusk, with a light on in the living room window. I got out, walked to the door, and knocked.

Nothing.

I knocked again, then stepped off the porch and walked to the garage. I was about to look for a window to see if any cars were in the garage when I heard the drum of horse's hooves. I walked around the side of the garage just in time to see a woman on a chestnut horse disappear behind the garage.

Jennifer?

I sneaked along the side of the garage and peeked around the corner. I saw a shed, and down a dirt lane, a fenced-in corral connected to a large red barn. The woman had dismounted, and was leading the horse through a gate into the riding area. She closed the gate and walked the horse through a large barn door.

I trotted past the shed, down the dirt lane, and up to the fence. I decided not to holler at Jennifer, in case she decided to ride off – or run me down on her horse. I climbed over the fence, hurried up to the barn door, and looked inside. Several horses were in stalls, but I didn't see Jennifer, so I took a couple of steps into the barn. I ignored the smells of hay, manure, and horses and looked around. I didn't see Jennifer, but I spotted an open door on the other side of the barn. I went over to it and poked my head out.

This side of the barn had a long porch, and Jennifer was sitting on a rocker. She wore tan riding slacks, a white blouse, and riding boots. All looked as expensive as the gold jewelry she seemed so fond of. A tall glass sat on a small table next to her.

"Hello," I said as I stepped out the door.

She leaped out of the rocker with a curse and took a few steps backward. Then she recognized me. "I thought I told you I didn't want to talk to you," she snapped. She started to step off the porch, leaving the glass behind. "My husband is at a meeting, but I'm going to call him. You better hightail it out of here this time. If he finds you here, he's not going to be happy."

"Wait," I called out. "I found Marcia, but then she disappeared. I think she might be in danger."

She halted and slowly turned around.

"You talked to Marcia?" she asked softly. A hand fiddled with a small gold cross necklace.

I nodded as I took a few steps toward her. "A few days ago."

Her mouth opened, but it took a moment for her to get any words out. "How is she?" she finally murmured.

"She *was* fine. Now I'm not so sure." I leaned against the railing. "Has she tried to contact you?"

She looked out into the deepening twilight and said, "I haven't talked to Marcia since she left town, almost thirty years ago."

"Why not?"

"She didn't want me to." Pain flashed across her face. "She said she was making a clean break, from Sagebrush, from our family. From my father. I never knew where she went."

"I thought you two were close. Didn't she look up to you?"

"Maybe at one time. By the time she had the baby, she was angry with the entire family."

"When she was pregnant, did you try to help her?"

"How?" She crossed her arms defensively. "My father was in control of everything, and Ben, my husband, didn't want to challenge him." She bent her head. "I ended up being the big sister who wasn't able to protect her from anyone. All I could do was be there to comfort her, but she didn't want that."

"After Marcia left town, did you ever try to contact her?"

"My father told me not to, that if I did, there would be con-sequences."

"He'd take all this," I waved a hand to encompass the barn and land, "away from you and your husband."

"A trust bought the land, but that's all." She wrapped her arms around herself. "You don't understand. I had no choice but to let Marcia go. She wanted it that way, and if I hadn't, my father would've found ways to punish me."

"Like what?"

"He has his ways." Then her head jerked up. "And do you think Ben would be sheriff if my father didn't want him to be? Being a lawman is everything to Ben. I couldn't let my father take that away, and he would have if I'd tried to get in touch with Marcia."

"You and Ben could've gone somewhere else."

"Sagebrush is all we know. We could never move." She mustered up some defiance. "You need to go. Do you know what would happen if my father heard I was talking to a private investigator?"

"Why would he care?"

"He cares about everything in this town."

"If Marcia calls you, let me know." I tried to hand her my business card, but like Annette, she wouldn't take it.

"If Marcia contacts me," she said, "you'd be the last person I'd tell."

"Even if it might help her?"

Tears welled up in her eyes. "You'd better go," she repeated.

She turned and rushed past me and into the barn. I walked slowly around the barn and back down the dirt lane. Somewhere far off, I heard a tractor in a field, a farmer cutting alfalfa in the cool of the evening. It was peaceful out here, so different from the hustle and bustle of a big city. Yet the turmoil of life made no distinction between the two.

Dusk had turned to darkness by the time I made my way around the house and to my car. I drove down the dirt road and onto County Road 15, my headlights cutting a swath in front of me. I reached the highway, thinking about Mayor Holder and what would make a man become so controlling of his family. A semi passed me, and I realized I was going too slowly. I sped up, my mind still elsewhere.

A car passed going the other way, and for a brief moment, I was alone on the highway. I crested a small hill and crossed over a bridge. Then headlights appeared as small dots in my rearview mirror, but they grew larger by the second.

"That guy's flying," I muttered to no one.

For a second, I wondered whether a cop had been waiting by the bridge and had clocked me speeding. I glanced at the speedometer. I was going five over the limit. Speeding, yes, but worthy of a ticket? Hardly.

I eased up on the gas until I was going the speed limit. The head-lights drew closer. I peered into the rearview mirror, trying to see if it was a cop car. It didn't look like it, but the newer cruisers had flat lights on top, so it was harder to recognize them. I sucked in a breath and braced myself for flashing lights that didn't come.

Suddenly the car moved into the lane next to me. It sped up, and then it veered toward me but didn't make contact with the 4-Runner.

"Hey!" I spun the steering wheel, surprised.

I took a quick look into the car – a dark, four-door sedan – but I couldn't see the driver. I pulled harder to the right. My right wheels skidded onto the shoulder. The car stayed close to my side. I felt the 4-Runner skid and I slammed on the brakes. My tires squealed, then the 4-Runner dipped and I was suddenly careening off the road toward a barbed wire fence. I finally screeched to a stop, slammed forward and bumped my head against the visor.

I flew out of the car and looked to the highway. All I saw of the car were red taillights. They faded and winked out. I cursed, then stumbled to the front of the 4-Runner. I'd come within inches of crashing through the fence. I checked the car, but there didn't appear to be any damage, so I got in and backed up. When I reached the highway, I drove carefully back into town, alert for the sedan. I meandered up and down the quiet streets, but didn't see it. I passed a few bars, but the sedan wasn't at any of them, either. I finally gave up and went back to the Sagebrush Inn.

The night clerk stared at me as I marched through the lobby and to my room. I let myself in, pushed the bathroom door open with a bang, turned on the light, and checked my head in the mirror. I had a small bump right at my hairline. No big deal. Thank goodness – I didn't want to have to explain a bruise to Willie. Just then, my phone rang. I checked the caller.

"Were your ears burning?" I said when I picked up.

"What?" Willie asked.

"I was just thinking of you."

"All good thoughts, right?"

"Uh-huh." I glanced at the bump, then turned off the light and strolled into the bedroom.

"Catch me up," she said.

As I sat down on the bed, I told her everything that had happened since we'd last talked. When I finished, she said, "Yeah, Gina told me the other day she hadn't heard from her mother, but then she's been on a different shift and I haven't seen her. Do you think someone's hurt Marcia?"

"I hope not."

"Me, too."

"It's interesting the hold Mayor Holder has on these people." I said. "They're scared to death of him, and yet somehow he's managed to *stay* mayor for all these years. According to some people, he's a horrible guy, but he's fooled everyone all this time."

"It's possible. I had to take a seminar at the hospital on domestic violence, and they discussed a doctor who had a great reputation in the medical community, but his wife and children recorded him at home. He was vicious, and screamed and yelled at them. He was two different men, like Jekyll and Hyde."

"Huh."

"So be careful, hon, okay? Mayor Holder may be that type of guy."

"I will."

We talked for a little while longer, and then we said goodbye. I sat for a while, gazing around the room. It didn't seem like anyone had been in the room *this* time, but I still had a creepy feeling.

Then I thought about the incident on the highway. The driver had been careful not to hit the 4-Runner, as if he'd wanted to cause me trouble without damaging his car. If the driver lived in Sagebrush, he – or she – could be worried I'd see the car. Smart move.

I'd barely been back in town and already I'd been run off the road. Things were unraveling for someone in this small town. I just didn't know who.

# CHAPTER NINETEEN

I watched TV for a while, and then my phone rang.

"You really upset my father," Gina Smith said when I answered.

"What'd he say?"

"He's still angry I dredged all this up, and he doesn't think you should be asking any questions. The only thing he seemed worried about was whether something had happened to my mother."

"That's interesting," I said.

"I hope you get to the bottom of this."

"I will," I said, with more confidence than I felt. "I'll call you soon."

"Thanks."

I put my phone on the nightstand and went to bed. I tossed and turned, then fell into a fitful sleep. Sometime in the night, a large truck parked outside, the groan of its engine waking me. I checked the time: one a.m. I fell asleep again. In my dreams, someone kept coming into my room. I finally got up, showered, and went into the hotel dining room. A few truckers were at one of the tables, eating and talking to one another. I sat nearby, ordered coffee, and thought about my next move. I decided it was time to see Mayor Holder. However, it was too early to pay him a visit just yet, so I ordered eggs and bacon, a breakfast I usually never made for myself. When it arrived, I ate slowly and read the local paper. In it I saw an ad for Holder Farm Equipment. The store was located on Tenth Street, wherever that was. I would drop by there after my visit with Toby's father.

I finished my meal, paid, and went out to the front desk. The young clerk was in his usual spot, but his video game wasn't on. He was slouched in his chair, looking off into space. He had dark circles under sleepy eyes, and he looked a little pale. Too much partying the night before?

"Could you tell me where Mayor Holder's office is?" I asked.

He jumped, then said, "Uh, he's out at the dairy plant."

"And that's where exactly?"

"Follow Main Street west. It'll keep going, and the plant is about five miles out of town. You can't miss it."

"Thanks."

I went back to my room and grabbed my backpack with my laptop, then walked outside. I took a deep breath of the fresh air and went to the 4-Runner. I gave it a once-over in the daylight, and didn't notice any further damage. With a relieved sigh, I got in and drove out to Holder Dairy.

» » » » »

The Holder Dairy plant was a series of large white buildings that sat a hundred yards off the road. I took the only road onto the property, and found a parking space in front of a small building with a sign that read, "Office." A steady rumble of machinery greeted me as I got out and went inside.

The office was plain and simple, with white walls, a sofa against the far wall, and windows that looked out into the parking lot. A hallway led to other offices, and the murmur of voices drifted out to me. A woman about my age sat at a metal desk, working at a computer. She looked up and smiled at me.

"May I help you?"

"I'd like to speak to Mayor Holder," I said.

"He's not in."

I jerked my head at the sofa. "I can wait."

Just then her phone rang. She picked it up, listened, and frowned. When she finished, she replaced the receiver and eyed me carefully. "The mayor won't be in until this afternoon."

I glanced toward the hall. Was someone watching us, and had that someone warned her about me?

"It's rather important that I speak with him," I said as I gazed surreptitiously at the ceiling, searching for a hidden camera. "Do you know where he is?"

"No." Now she was cool. "And he'll be busy later today."

She didn't offer to let me make an appointment, and I didn't bother asking. I was sure she'd tell me his schedule was full.

"I'll come back another time," I said.

"You do that." There was no warmth in her tone.

I gave her my most amiable smile – which did nothing – and left. I wondered if I should've tried the Bogie approach, played it dark and surly. But that probably wouldn't have helped. I sat in the parking lot and waited for Holder to show his face, but after a while, the secretary came out and gave me a hard look. I waved, started the 4-Runner, and drove off. I reached the main road and parked down from the dairy entrance, watching for Holder's black Cadillac. After an hour, this seemed pointless, and I worried that the longer I stayed, the more I risked drawing a visit from the sheriff. And I wasn't ready to see him yet. I decided to move on before someone figured out what I was doing.

Since I'd drawn a blank here, I decided to try Toby Holder. I sat for a moment in the 4-Runner and pulled up a map of Sagebrush. I studied it and quickly found Tenth Street. Holder Farm Equipment was at the opposite end of town from where I was. I fired up the 4-Runner, got back on the road, and was soon driving down Tenth Street.

Toby Holder's store was a big green warehouse on a large corner lot. Behind the building, a lot surrounded by a high chain-link fence was full of all sorts of large tractors and tractor attachments, some new, some used. A few trucks were parked in front of the warehouse.

I pulled in next to a beat-up blue pickup, went inside, and glanced around. Smaller farm equipment was displayed all around the store, along with other accessories and tools. Two men stood near a riding lawn mower, talking to a salesman. Standing at a long counter at the back of the store was a man with blond hair and a handlebar mustache. Annette's husband. He wore a blue T-shirt with "Bill" on it, and was helping a young farmer in worn jeans and a plaid shirt. As they talked, the young man kept adjusting his John Deere cap. They completed an order, and the young man paid and left.

Bill looked at me with a smile. "What can I do for you?"

I moseyed up to the counter. "Is Toby around?"

Just then, a tall, solidly built man in new Wranglers and a T-shirt similar to Bill's walked up. The name on his shirt read "Toby."

"I'm –" I started to introduce myself.

"I know who you are," Toby said. His voice was deep, with a gruff edge. "Jennifer called me."

"Are you going to give me the cold shoulder, too?" I asked.

Bill's eyes darted between us. I wondered if he recognized me from last night.

Toby shook his head. "I don't have anything to tell you."

One of the men inspecting the riding lawn mower headed up to the counter, so Toby stepped away. I moved with him.

"I'm trying to find your sister Marcia," I said. "Have you heard from her in the last few days?"

"Nope, and if I had, I wouldn't tell you. Now –" he began in a low voice.

"Let me guess," I interrupted, "you're going to tell me to mind my own business, and that your father's a mean man, and to leave him alone."

His lips were a thin line that hardly moved when he talked. "He had a hard upbringing, and he's made good here in spite of it, so I'm not going to fault him for that." He stood staring at me, his stance wide. "What're you doing here?"

"I told you, I'm trying to find Marcia, and everything points to Sagebrush. But nobody wants to give me a straight answer about anything. I find that a little bit suspicious, wouldn't you?"

He glared at me, but didn't say anything.

I nodded. "Okay, I'll try your father next."

"Don't bother him."

"Try and stop me."

"You're not going to get anything from him."

"Why? Is he hiding something?"

"There's nothing to hide," he barked. "Just because my father handled things a certain way a long time ago doesn't mean he did any-thing wrong."

"He forced his daughter to leave her boyfriend and return here. And he threatened to force her to give the baby up for adoption."

The other men in the store were trying hard to appear as if they weren't listening.

Toby lowered his voice again. "So?"

"Who'd he send to get her?"

"I don't know. Some of his pals, I guess. I don't know what happened that night."

"Did you ever meet Marcia's boyfriend?"

His eyes darted away. "No."

I crossed my arms casually. "Now why don't I believe you?"

"You can believe what you want. I didn't know the guy, but he shouldn't have gotten her pregnant."

"I hear he didn't."

He scrutinized me. "What do you know?"

I shrugged. "I don't know." I could play his game. We had a staring contest. Then I said, "Tell me about your friend Jay."

His eyebrows arched in surprise. "Where did you hear that name?"

"Nowhere."

He glanced over at Bill, who was helping his customer and very deliberately not paying attention to us. Toby looked back at me.

"Jay's death was an accident."

"I hear it might've been a drug deal gone bad," I said. "You know anything about that?"

"You can believe what you want." Toby gestured out the door. "You need to get in your car and head on out of town."

"I like it here." I grinned at him. "I think I'll stay for a while, maybe move here. It's such a pleasant, friendly town."

Toby's eyes narrowed. "Get out of here."

"I'm going to find Marcia," I said. "If you know where she is, you better tell me."

"Your little private investigator's license doesn't hold much weight here," he sneered. Then he stormed away.

I felt the eyes of Bill and the customers on me as I sauntered out the door. I stood in the sunlight and mulled over the conversation. Toby Holder hadn't told me a lot with words, but he'd revealed more than he'd intended. I was sure he knew something about John Smith. When Marcia and John had their secret liaisons, had Toby known about them? Had he seen them together, and told Mayor Holder about it? Not only that, I was sure Toby had been talking to the sheriff. How else would he have known I had a private investigator's license? I hadn't actually shown the license to anyone but the sheriff.

Toby was hiding something, but what did that have to do with Marcia? If I could answer that, I'd bet my private investigator's license I'd find Marcia.

# CHAPTER TWENTY

At this point, I needed to talk to the one man everyone said I shouldn't: Mayor Holder. But how could I find him? I didn't relish the idea of staking out the dairy plant to wait for him to arrive, especially since I might draw the attention of the sheriff. And what if the mayor never showed today? My next bet was to find out where he lived and try there. Then my phone rang. I checked the number, but didn't recognize it.

"Hello?" I answered tentatively.

"Reed Ferguson?"

"Yes." The voice seemed familiar, as if I'd heard it before.

"Mayor Holder."

I glanced around, wondering if I really was in a *Twilight Zone* episode. "How did you get my number?" I asked.

"I have my ways." He sounded very much like me when I didn't want to reveal how I got information. "I want to talk to you, son. Meet me at the park on Main Street, now."

I was tempted to tell him no, just to screw with him, but he hung up before I could say another word. I pocketed my phone, then wondered what I was about to get into. Was this a trap of some kind? Would the mayor resort to something nefarious in order to get me to stop asking questions? I shrugged. I'd be careful, but there was no way I was *not* going to meet him. I went to the 4-Runner, and as I headed out of the parking lot, I saw Toby Holder standing in the warehouse door, watching me.

» » » » »

I drove down Main Street a few minutes later, and in the center of town I noticed a black Cadillac parked prominently in front of a park that took up an entire square block. The park had a pavilion in the center, lots of tall maple trees, and benches all around. A few people were in the pavilion, eating sack lunches at picnic tables. I started down a path toward them when I spotted a man sitting at one end of a bench near Main Street. A tree towered over him, providing some shade. I walked casually over and stared at him.

He gestured with a wrinkled hand toward the other end of the bench. "Please, have a seat."

I hesitated, just long enough so he'd know I wasn't taking an order, then sat down and took a second to study him. Alvin Holder was tall, like his son, but where Toby was solid muscle, Mayor Holder had withered with age. But he still had strength in his face, and his eyes flashed dangerously. He looked dapper, if somewhat out of style, in white slacks and suit vest, with a light blue shirt and black tie. It was hot, even in the shade, but he wasn't sweating. A woman walked by with her dog, and he smiled at her and said it was a nice day. They exchanged a few pleasantries and then she waved and walked off. Then he turned to me.

"I've lived in Sagebrush since 1963," he said as he fanned himself with a Panama hat. He sounded like his son, the same deep, gruff voice. "I started a small dairy and built it into something. I had to expand, up to hundreds of acres now. We make sweet cream, condensed milk, and nonfat dry milk, which are all used to make cheese, yogurt, and ice cream." It sounded like a commercial: well-rehearsed and delivered with just the right amount of sales pitch to impress me. Only I wasn't. "Holder Dairy may not be as big as some other plants," he went on, "but I've turned it into something. I may sell it soon, to a bigger dairy. That'll be a windfall for the city. The dairy already helps our economy here immensely, but expanding the dairy would mean more jobs, and it'll help the community in other ways."

"And you'll benefit plenty yourself."

The hat stopped for a second, and then he resumed fanning himself. "That's true," he finally said.

A man in blue slacks and a striped shirt walked by. He nodded his head at the mayor and smiled.

"Afternoon, Don." Not to be outdone, the mayor gave him a big smile of his own.

Don said hello, and the mayor interrupted our talk to chat with him. I was well aware of what Holder was doing. He wanted me to see him as the man of the people, the guy who provided jobs for the town, a well-respected leader of the community. A good guy.

I found myself momentarily falling for it. Was everyone lying about him? Then I thought about what Willie had said last night about domestic violence. Was Holder like the doctor she'd talked about, a Jekyll and Hyde character?

Don moved on and Holder cleared his throat. "You sure like stirring up trouble."

He thought he'd buttered me up, and now we were getting to it.

"I want to know where your daughter Marcia is," I said.

"She showed up at my house."

I tried not to show my surprise. "When?"

"Last night. I was watching TV in the den and she just appeared. I haven't seen her in years." He showed no emotion.

"What did she want?"

"She thought I'd sent people after her, but why would I do that now?"

"You weren't in Denver recently?"

He shook his head. "I haven't been there since last fall, when I had some meetings downtown."

"You didn't check on her while you were there?"

"I did not."

"It looks like there was trouble at her house."

He gave me an approving look. "So you've been there."

"Yes." I told him about the broken lamp and blood. "I thought maybe she'd been taken against her will."

"Well, we know that's not true."

"If I can believe you."

Irritation crossed his face, then was gone. "She's okay."

"Did she tell you what happened at her house? Maybe she was assaulted, then escaped, and came up here."

"She didn't tell me a thing."

"Did she tell you where she's staying?"

"I don't know. We spoke for a minute, and then she vanished as quietly as she'd appeared. I continued watching TV."

An indifferent chill emanated from him, but then one of the lunch-time crowd walked by and the mayor chatted briefly with her, all warmth and charisma.

"What else did she talk to you about?" I asked when the woman left.

"She asked about that night in Kansas. She seems to think that whatever happened back then is rearing its ugly head now. I told her that's ridiculous."

"The night you came for her."

He hesitated, then nodded.

"What'd you tell her?" I asked.

"I had to do what I thought was best. Her actions had caused me a lot of problems."

I had a hard time not letting my anger boil over. He was so calm about the whole thing, so righteous. He gave no thought to anyone but himself.

"Why'd you bring her back?" I asked. "Why not just let her go?"

"I had a reputation in town. I couldn't let people think I wasn't capable of handling my own family. This was – is – a good community, churchgoing folk."

"You worried about what Pastor Sheehan would say."

"That's part of it. Marcia had no idea what she'd done to my wife, either. The embarrassment. The disappointment. And I wasn't going to have Marcia running off with some hoodlum."

"You knew who she was dating?"

"No. Hoodlum's just a figure of speech."

"Was it Toby's friend Jay?"

"No."

"You're sure."

"Jay got what was coming to him."

"Huh," I said. He didn't think much of Jay. "Did you have something to do with his death?"

"No."

"What's Jay's last name?"

"I don't remember." He said it too quickly to be believed. His eyes narrowed. "Who my daughter was seeing is a mystery to me. Satisfied?"

I wasn't, but he wasn't going to say more about it, so I moved on. "What happened in that hotel room?"

He shrugged. "I wasn't there."

I raised my eyebrows. "She remembers your voice."

"She had a concussion, and she's mixed up about a lot of things that happened that night."

I wasn't sure I believed that. "Who'd you send then?"

"Some people of mine. I was at a mayor's conference in Cleveland."

"I'll check."

"Please do. I'm not lying."

"People who kidnapped –" I had to search for the correct name. "Victoria?"

He shrugged. "I wish I knew. It was all a long time ago." And suddenly, our meeting was over. He stood up, put his hat on, and adjusted it carefully. "You've talked to me now. I think it's time you leave town quietly. I'd hate to get tough with you."

"I hear you're good at being tough."

He threw me a wicked smile. "Don't make things difficult for yourself."

"I'm not leaving until I know Marcia's safe."

Mayor Holder contemplated me for a moment, then strolled off without another word. He never once looked back at me. I sat for a while, not quite sure what to make of my conversation with him. My gut said he was telling the truth about Marcia's visit, but not about whatever had happened years ago. And if Marcia was asking him about the past, it meant she didn't think he was being truthful, either. Another thought occurred to me. Was Marcia wrapped up in whatever had happened? Had *she* been lying to me?

I shook my head in disgust, and my thoughts turned back to Mayor Holder. He was smooth, but underneath that veneer was a coldness like I'd rarely felt before. I couldn't imagine growing up with that kind of father. It made me grateful for what I had. I thought of my own father, a man who was quiet and could be gruff, but who undoubtedly loved me. I suddenly pulled my phone out, found a number, and called it.

"Reed, dear?" my mother said. "What a pleasant surprise. How are you?"

"I'm fine, Mother. I just wanted to say hello."

"Is everything okay?"

"Yes. I … wanted to tell you that I love you, and thank you for all you've done for me."

"Now I know something's wrong. Did someone hit you on the head?"

And there she went in her high-pitched voice! She was a classic worrier. She used to worry that I was doing drugs, and that I'd never marry. I'd finally put those two concerns to bed, and now she was always nudging about when Willie and I would give her grandchildren.

"Mother, I'm fine."

"Are you sure? You don't sound good."

"I'm fine," I repeated.

"How's Willie? Are you two thinking about grandchildren?"

"Mother, we've only been married a few months."

"I know, but I can dream. Dear, why are you calling?"

"I realized I don't tell you how much you mean to me. And Dad, too."

"Well." She sniffed, and not in a miffed kind of way. "That's very sweet of you, dear."

"Is Dad there? I'd like to tell him the same thing."

"He's golfing, but I'll tell him what you said."

"That would be great, but I'll call later, too."

We chatted for a few minutes longer. Then I told her I loved her and ended the call. I could picture her on the deck of their Florida condo. She had probably set the phone down and fainted. Or called the police, or Willie, thinking something was *definitely* wrong with me.

My stomach grumbled, and I decided that before I did anything else, I'd get some lunch. I pushed myself off the bench and walked to Main Street, then down the block to the Main Street Café.

## CHAPTER TWENTY-ONE

The lunch crowd at the café was in full swing, but I was able to get a booth near the back, where I could watch the entrance. I had a sneaky feeling that Mayor Holder had someone spying on me, and I took comfort in the shadows near the kitchen. I ordered a meatball sub, and while I waited for it, I pulled out my phone and called Ace.

"Anything to report?" I asked.

"No one has come or gone from Marcia Holder's house," he said.

I heard a feminine voice in the background. "Who're you talking to?"

"Mrs. Pratt."

"Who?"

"Marcia's next-door-neighbor."

"Oh, Doris." I slapped my palm on my forehead. "Is she giving you a hard time about being there?"

"No, she saw me sitting in my car and she asked me if I wanted some lemonade, and then she said I could wait on her front porch. So I sat with her and we talked. She's real nice and said she enjoys the company. When Deuce came over last night, she gave us dessert and taught us how to play gin rummy." He lowered his voice. "It's not as fun as pool, but it's okay."

I smiled. Leave it to the Goofballs to turn a stakeout into card-playing fun. And it sounded like Doris was delighted with them. They had that effect on people.

"But you're still watching the house?"

"Yes. I'll call if I see anyone. You don't need to check on me, Reed. I know what I'm doing."

Did he sound a little short with me, like Doris had been with me? Was she already rubbing off on him?

"Okay, you're doing a great job," I said.

"When are you coming home?"

"I'm not sure yet. Keep an eye on Willie and the condo, too, okay?"

"Are you expecting trouble?"

"No, but it pays to be careful."

"Will do. I need to go. Mrs. Pratt brought me some cookies."

I laughed, thanked him, and ended the call. After a while, the waitress brought me a Coke and my meatball sub. I had just started on it when a man in gray slacks and a green polo shirt entered the café. A hush fell over the room. He took off sunglasses, surveyed the room, then strode over to my table.

"May I help you?" I said through a mouthful of meatball sub.

"Pastor Sheehan," he introduced himself.

I swallowed hard, the bite stuck in my throat. I set down my sandwich and gulped some Coke. "What can I do for you?"

He gestured at the seat across from me. "May I?"

Ah, we were both so polite. I broke that with, "Knock yourself out." That's how Bogie would've handled it.

He slid into the booth and laid his soft hands, which obviously had never seen hard labor, on the table. He was older, maybe in his seventies like Mayor Holder, with lightly tanned skin, a square face, wavy brown hair with a little too much gel in it, and eyes set a little too closely together. He was fit, in a gym kind of way, not from working the land. My first impression was that he was trying too hard for a GQ-casual look. He contemplated me for a long time, so I took another bite of sandwich.

"They make great food," I said. "Have you eaten here?"

He nodded, and as if by magic, the waitress came over with a sandwich and a cup of coffee for him.

"Thank you, Betty," he said to her.

"You're welcome, Pastor Sheehan." She moved off quickly, as if she was almost afraid of him.

"Do you always get that kind of service?" I asked.

Sheehan tapped his fingertips together and waited dramatically. "Let's cut to the chase. We have a nice community here, good people who work hard. They don't want trouble, but you've come into town, stirring things up."

"You're the second person who's said that to me today." *Just a little bit ago*, I thought.

"It's time you leave town."

"I want to know that Marcia Holder is safe, and then I'll gladly go home."

"I'm sure she's fine."

"Have you seen her recently?"

"Not for years."

"She showed up at Mayor Holder's house last night."

"I heard."

"But he has no idea where she went," I said. "Or he may have done something to her."

He frowned. "Mayor Holder wouldn't hurt his daughter."

"He did, years ago, by the way he treated her. He forced her to come back home when she didn't want to."

"She's fine," he repeated.

"You don't know that."

He ignored that. "Why are you asking about something that happened thirty years ago?"

"Are we talking about Marcia's pregnancy, her running away and being forced back here by her father, or her baby's kidnapping?"

He stared hard at me, but didn't respond.

"I'll take that as a yes to all," I said. I don't know why I was being such a smartass. I guess I was getting tired of the weirdness from everyone in town.

"None of it has any relevance today."

"How do you know? Even Marcia's been asking questions about those events."

"I just know."

I shook my head. "Sorry, that's not good enough for me."

The fingertips kept tapping together. Around us, people talked quietly, but those I could see were trying to listen in. Our waitress a-voided our table, but she was watching from afar.

"That was a difficult time for the family," he said quietly. "I spent a lot of time with Mrs. Holder, counseling her through her grief."

"What about Marcia? I'm sure she was grieving."

He sighed. "She refused to talk to me."

"What did Mayor Holder think of her situation?"

He chose his words carefully. "He was not pleased. But I doubt many fathers would have been happy that their high-school-aged daughter got pregnant. Certainly not at that time. And he's the mayor in a small town. A lot of people look up to him as an example."

"And he should have the perfect family."

"I didn't say that."

"Did you know that when he brought Marcia home, he beat her, and then kept her as a prisoner in his home?"

His cool demeanor threatened to crack. "I wasn't aware of that."

I leaned back and crossed my arms. "I hear you were none too happy about Marcia's predicament as well. What would the community say about one of your members getting herself into that kind of situation? You were worried about how it reflected on you."

"I only want the best for the people here."

"What about Jennifer and Toby? Were you there to help them?"

"Jennifer was married, and didn't need my counseling. Toby, on the other hand … he was naturally upset when the baby was kidnapped, and then to have his friend die so soon after that."

"Tell me about Jay. What was his last name?"

"That was a very unfortunate business," he said, without telling me Jay's last name. "I don't want to speak ill of the dead, but he was trouble. He led a lot of boys in this town down a wrong path."

"Including Toby."

Sheehan nodded. "He was devastated by Jay's death, but in the end, it was best for Toby. It scared him straight. He cleaned himself up, got involved with farm equipment, and opened his store. He's done very well for himself." He grimaced. "You know that Jay was involved with drugs."

"So I heard."

"It's true. He was a mess. Couldn't keep a job, got some DUIs, who knows what else. I don't know how his wife put up with him."

"What was her name?"

"Paula. I think she was embarrassed by him, but she didn't have a job and was dependent on him. After his murder, she left town without saying a word to anyone. Just took off without her belongings and disappeared."

I uncrossed my arms and leaned forward. "When was this?"

"A few weeks after Jay was killed."

"How do you know something bad didn't happen to her, if she vanished without a trace?"

"The sheriff's department checked into it, and found nothing that suggested foul play."

I looked him in the eye, and he firmly met my gaze. "Who are you covering for?"

"No one."

"I'm not sure I believe you."

He was taken aback. "I'm a man of God."

"That doesn't mean you can't be lying."

His face twitched as he tried to control himself. I wondered if anyone had ever challenged him before.

"What did Paula look like?" I asked.

"Oh." He let out a breath and thought about it. "She was a small woman, petite, with curly brown hair. She was friendly, and cute. Even though she was married, Toby had a crush on her. He had a hard time when she left, especially with it coming right after that business with Jay. Why do you ask?"

"Some skeletal remains were found not too long ago in a field near

Woodrow. Based on the small size of the bones, they think it was a petite woman, and they guess she may have been buried in that field about thirty years ago." I was fudging on the time frame, but I wanted to see his reaction.

He paled. "What a coincidence."

"You think?" I let sarcasm drip from my voice.

"Paula left town after Jay's death," he said.

I remembered what the mayor had said to me about Jay getting what he deserved. "What if Mayor Holder didn't like Jay's influence on his son and the rest of the kids in this town?"

"Meaning what?"

"You know the rumors about Mayor Holder?"

"Like?" he asked evasively.

I cocked an eyebrow. "He's not the nice man everyone thinks he is."

He didn't answer at first. "He can get angry," he finally said. "O-ver the years, I've tried to get him to look inward, but he's a stubborn man."

"Could he get angry enough to kill?"

"Kill who?"

"Jay and his wife."

"What for?"

I shrugged. "I don't know."

My conclusion was a bit of a stretch, but Sheehan's reaction was intriguing. His face contorted into a mixture of confusion and doubt.

"I don't like what you're suggesting. I'm sure Marcia is fine, and you're doing nothing good here with your questions. Leave the past in the past." He sounded eerily like John Smith.

"Did Marcia know something about the deaths of Jay and his wife?" I asked.

"No."

"How do you know?"

He shrugged. "I don't. It was a guess."

"What are you hiding?"

"Nothing." He laid his palms back down on the table. "I've worked very hard to get where I am. I love this town, and the people here need me, and I won't have you jeopardize that." He slid out of the booth and stood up. "You shouldn't accuse me of anything. Take my advice and leave town."

"When I find Marcia, I'll go," I said.

He turned and greeted a few people as he walked out of the café. A few didn't look as if they were particularly fond of him, let alone as if they needed him, but they were striving for friendliness. Did they need to appear as if they liked him, to avoid consequences from Mayor Holder? Or something else? I glanced across the table. The pastor had left his sandwich and coffee untouched. I wondered if I would have to pay for them.

I started to take another bite of my sandwich, but I'd lost my appetite. I didn't know what to make of Pastor Sheehan. I couldn't tell whether or not he was lying to me, and he had seemed anything but surprised by my suggestion that Mayor Holder might've killed Jay and his wife, Paula. I wondered if I'd just discovered the identity of the skeletal remains in the field in Woodrow. Did Sheehan suspect Holder of Paula's murder, and did her death, and Jay's, have something to do with Mayor Holder, or someone else in town? Maybe Pastor Sheehan? That could explain his insistence that I stop poking around for answers.

I pushed my plate away, thinking that the more they tried to scare me off, the more determined I was to stay until I found Marcia, preferably safe and sound.

## CHAPTER TWENTY-TWO

I paid for my meal – they didn't charge me for Sheehan's uneaten sandwich – and I drove back to the Sagebrush Inn. I wanted to see if Mayor Holder was telling the truth about being in Cleveland the night his daughter was brought home from Kansas, and I wanted to learn more about Jay, who had been murdered around that same time. When I walked into the lobby, my favorite clerk was at the counter, but this time he was typing away on his cellphone.

"No video games today?" I asked as I leaned my arms on the counter.

He finished typing and put the phone down. "Huh?"

"Never mind. Do you have a second?" Of course he did. I doubted he ever experienced a real work rush during the afternoon.

"Uh, sure."

"There was a guy named Jay who was murdered here in 1985."

"Yeah, I remember hearing something about that."

"Do you know his last name?"

He shook his head. "That was before my time. All I know was they thought it was drug dealers put a hit on him, or something like that."

"Who's they?"

"Huh?"

Man, he'd fit right in with the Goofballs. "Who said it was drug dealers?"

"I don't know, I'm just telling you what I heard."

I smiled. "Okay, thanks."

"You staying another night?"

I nodded and paid. "Any other guests right now?"

"No. We mostly get truckers, and it picks up during the fair."

"When is that?"

"July."

I thanked him again, went to my room, and looked around. Everything appeared exactly as I'd left it. If anyone had been in this morning, I couldn't tell. I got out my laptop, sat down on the bed, and began an internet search on Mayor Alvin Holder. I found the same articles I had before, so this time, I narrowed my search by adding "Cleveland." I checked a few pages of results, and found that there was a conference of mayors that met annually in cities across the United States. But I couldn't find if they'd met in Cleveland. I continued with other search criteria, and finally found a brochure that someone had posted on a Pinterest page. It was for the 1985 Conference of Mayors, hosted by the city of Cleveland. It also listed conference speakers for the event, and surprisingly enough, one of them was Mayor Alvin Holder of Sagebrush, Colorado, speaking on the economy of small town agriculture. I found an online calendar for 1985 and checked the dates of the conference, then compared those to the date I remembered being on Gina's birth certificate. The conference was the same week that she'd been born.

"Bingo," I said out loud.

That confirmed Mayor Holder hadn't been in Russell, Kansas, the night Marcia had been brought back to Sagebrush. But why did she seem so sure her father had been there? I sat back and stared at the ceiling, then suddenly snapped my fingers. Marcia had said that her father and Toby were the spitting image of each other. I'd seen them both, and I'd agree. But not only did they look alike, they *sounded* alike. What if Toby had been sent to Kansas to bring his sister back? If that was the case, why hadn't Mayor Holder, John Smith, or Toby told me that? I sat for a minute, mulling that over, then decided that I'd pay Toby Holder another visit and ask him.

I spent a few more minutes on the internet, looking for anything about Toby Holder. I found his bio on the site for Holder Farm Equipment, and a mention in a directory for the local Lodge, but nothing else. I did a quick White Pages search on him, and it appeared that he had never married and didn't have children. A map showed that he lived west of town, in what appeared to be a secluded area. Was Marcia holed up out there? I should check out his house as well. I shelved that idea for the moment and turned my search to the mysterious Jay whatever-his-last-name-was.

I typed Jay, 1985, and Sagebrush, Colorado into the search engine, but came up with nothing. I added "murder" and started poking through results. It took a bit of hunting, but I finally found a small article that mentioned the murder of Jay Overstrom, whose body had been found in a field east of Sagebrush. I filtered my search more, using "drugs" as a term, and came across another article with a bit more detail.

Jay Overstrom had moved to Sagebrush with his wife, Paula, in the early '80s. He was known around town as a rabble-rouser who drank too much and did drugs, much to the chagrin of Pastor Sheehan, who had been interviewed for the article. The article discussed Overstrom's history of arrests in Denver, mostly for domestic violence and possession of drugs, and his suspected connections to a drug-smuggling ring. Over-strom had been killed in gang fashion with a bullet to the back of the head. Because of Overstrom's history in Denver, and the manner in which he'd been shot, the authorities speculated that Overstrom might have been murdered by someone from the smuggling ring. At the time the article was written, no killer had been found.

It's what I'd heard from Annette Gessler, but now I had a name for his wife. I set the laptop beside me, grabbed my phone, and called Detective Spillman.

"You're calling me again so soon," she said in a clipped tone. "This can't be good news for me."

"Actually, it may be. Remember those skeletal remains I was asking you about?"

"That had been found in a field near Woodrow?"

"Right. Can you do a check on Paula Overstrom? The remains may be her."

"How do you know that?" She was genuinely curious now.

I told her about my investigation. "It's just a guess," I concluded.

"Not a bad one," she said. "I'll make a few phone calls about it. Good work, Ferguson."

I felt my face get hot. "Thanks."

"That really is all you need?"

"Yes."

"I'm shocked."

"I'm shocked myself. Two compliments from you in one conversation."

"Don't push your luck."

Then she was gone.

I pocketed my phone and was about to shut down my computer when the preview to an article caught my eye. I clicked on the link. It was an article from a newspaper in Texas. It had been written in 2005, and discussed some of the ways drugs flowed into the United States. One example was of a Pastor Miguel Mendoza from a small church in Mexico who had been accused of smuggling drugs across the border. He had ties to Mexican drug lords, and he'd been suspected of working with religious groups and leaders in small towns across Texas, Oklahoma, and Colorado, to distribute the drugs. The article ended by saying Mendoza was suspected in several murders of his accomplices, including a man known as "Jay-O."

I sat back, my mind racing. Was that why Pastor Sheehan hadn't wanted me to know Jay's last name? Had Sheehan been involved in a drug-smuggling operation with him?

"No," I said aloud. "That can't be."

But why not? It was worth checking out.

I shut down the laptop, put it in my backpack, and headed out to pay visits to Toby Holder and Pastor Sheehan. I had a lot more questions for both of them.

## CHAPTER TWENTY-THREE

It was almost four o'clock when I parked in front of Holder Farm Equipment. I hurried inside and glanced around. No customers were in the store, but Bill – Annette's husband – was behind the counter. When he saw me, he held up a hand.

"Toby said I'm not to let you in." He moved around the counter and ambled toward me.

"I want to ask him a few questions," I said.

He simultaneously shook his head and pointed toward the door. "Toby not's here, and you can't wait for him. Look, I don't want to get tough with you, mister, but you need to go, or I'll call the sheriff."

"Where is Toby?"

"He's with a customer, on site. Go on, now."

"All right, I'm going." I turned around and went back outside.

Bill stood at the entrance, stroking his handlebar mustache as he waited while I drove out of the parking lot. He was still there when I glanced in my rearview mirror a few seconds later. I sighed. Now what? I pulled over and yanked my phone out, then found Toby's home address. He lived a few miles outside of town. I'd wanted to check his house to make sure Marcia wasn't there, and what better time to do so than while he was still at work. I hit the gas and sped out of town.

Toby Holder's house was on a large lot surrounded by farmland. His property didn't have a fancy entrance like his sister Jennifer's ranch did, and his house wasn't nearly the size of hers, but it was every bit as nice. It was a two-story stone structure with an immense chimney. The front of the house faced south, with large windows to take in the view of rolling fields full of maize and sunsets, and a wide porch with a white railing. A three-car garage was on one side of the house, but I didn't see any cars around.

I got out and listened. A few mourning doves cooed, and then dead calm. A sudden vision sprung into my mind of Toby Holder standing inside the house, by a window, with a shotgun in his hand.

"Hello?" I called out in what I hoped was a cool voice.

Silence.

I took a deep, calming breath and walked slowly up a stone walkway, onto the front porch and up to a heavy wooden door. I couldn't find a doorbell, so I knocked loudly. I waited and rapped on the door again, not surprised that no one answered.

Toby was still working, right? I hoped so.

After knocking one final time, just to be sure, I tried a fancy doorknob. As I would've expected in a country home miles from a big city, it was unlocked. I turned the knob and let myself into Toby's house.

I tiptoed into an open foyer with a staircase to the left, and a living area directly in front of me. The décor was rustic, but everything was expensive, from leather couches, hardwood floors, a huge stone fire-place, and exposed beams. To the right of the foyer was an office with a large oak desk, floor-to-ceiling oak shelves with western knick knacks and some books that appeared brand new, and two paintings of cowboys on horses on one wall.

"Hello?" I called out again.

My voice echoed throughout the house. I stole through the living room and into a kitchen with shaker cabinets, black appliances, and granite countertops. It was tidy, with hardly any decorations. Around the corner was a den with a large TV, another leather couch, and two reclining chairs. Plush tan carpet had vacuum cleaner rows on it. Someone had recently cleaned. I moved to the right, down a short hallway to a storage room, then backpedaled and returned to the entryway.

I went into the office and checked out the desk. A laptop sat on it, but it was turned off. I booted it up, but it was password-protected, so I shut it off. I rummaged in the drawers. Besides the usual office supplies, I found the same article from the *Denver Post* that I'd read about the skeletal remains being found near Woodrow. What was Toby's interest in that?

I was pondering that when I thought I heard something. I listened, but after a moment, I figured I'd imagined it. I quietly shut the drawer, thinking I shouldn't waste more time. I hurried into the foyer and up the stairs. The second floor had two spare bedrooms, both with queen-sized beds, and a master suite decorated in masculine tones, with tan walls and a log bedroom set. I checked in dresser drawers and in the bathroom, but found nothing noteworthy, so I went back downstairs. I found stairs to the basement and called out. When no one answered, I quietly crept down.

If I'd expected a bogie man, I would've been disappointed. The basement consisted of a large TV room and a man cave. An odor of pungent smoke filled a room that held a pool table, pinball machine, and large bar. At the other end of the room was a cigar area, with more expensive furniture, and a walk-in humidor filled with a variety of what I assumed were very expensive cigars. On two of the walls in the main room, bottles of whiskey, bourbon, and tequila sat on glass shelves. I went to the shelves and scanned the bottles. One was a Highland Park 50-year-old single malt whiskey. I whistled.

"Over fifteen grand for that one," I muttered.

It wasn't the only pricey liquor on the shelves. Toby must have spent over a hundred grand on his liquor supply alone.

*The farm equipment business is better than good*, I thought.

Near the TV room was a bathroom, and beyond that a storage area. I went back to the stairs and took one final look around. Toby was living well. But I didn't see any signs of Marcia.

I sneaked back upstairs and found a door to the garage. Inside was a classic Corvette, two new Harleys, and an ATV. I checked them out, then peered through a window to the side of the house. Parked outside the garage was a large boat, and another newer pickup truck.

*Not bad.*

I didn't see anything else to note, so I stole back through the house and out the front door. Technically, I hadn't broken in, but I didn't think the sheriff would care about that. It was still some kind of illegal entry.

I stepped off the porch and walked around the house. In back was a small barn, but it was empty. No animals, and no Marcia. I finally concluded she wasn't around, and it was time to leave. I jogged back to the 4-Runner and drove away.

Once I neared the highway, I stopped and looked up Sheehan's address. He lived in town, near Annette Gessler. I didn't waste any time driving there, but when I arrived and knocked on the door, no one was home. I was tempted to see if Sheehan kept his door unlocked, but his neighbor was working in her flower garden. Strike illegal entry into his home. The woman eyed me as I walked back to my car.

"He's at church," she said in a gravelly voice.

"Thank you." I headed for my car, then turned back to her. "Where is that?"

She leaned back on her haunches. "The church? It's on Pine." Her tone said that I should've known. I smiled, but my face must've looked blank, because she pointed to the west. "Two blocks that way, then go north. You can't miss it."

I thanked her again, got in the 4-Runner, and followed her directions. Sagebrush Bible Church was a large white building on the corner. It was an older structure, with rectangular windows and a metal cross on top. A sign in front announced a Wednesday evening service at seven, and a service at ten on Sunday mornings.

*Today was Wednesday*, I thought.

A dark sedan was parked in a lot on the side of the building. I went over to the car, then walked around it. Was it the car that had run me off the road the other night? I couldn't tell.

I glanced around, then crossed a parched lawn to the church entrance and pulled open the door. The church was modest, with red carpet, hardwood pews on either side of a center aisle, and a small altar with a wooden podium. Behind it, a wooden cross dominated the wall. I spotted a door to the right of the altar and started down the aisle toward it. Then the door opened and Pastor Sheehan entered the sanctuary. He was now wearing a dark blue suit. He took a few steps and then saw me.

"What're you doing here?" he snapped.

"Overstrom. That's Jay's last name."

He gave me an appraising look. "Good for you."

"Why didn't you tell me his name? It would've been so much easier."

He shrugged. "What happened with Jay doesn't matter now. I'd hoped if I didn't tell you, you would give up and go home." He surveyed me up and down. "I see that didn't happen."

"Don't you care about Marcia?"

"Of course I do. I talked to the mayor, and he said she's fine."

I shook my head. "Holder doesn't know that, and he could be lying."

"Mayor Holder wouldn't do that. And Marcia had nothing to do with Jay Overstrom."

"How do you know?"

He shrugged. "He wasn't involved with her."

"He *was* involved in drugs."

"I know that."

I stared at him. "In my search, I found an interesting article about a Mexican pastor who was smuggling drugs into Colorado. He worked with religious groups and leaders to distribute the drugs."

"What're you saying?"

"Why cover up Overstrom's killing unless you have something to hide?"

He flew at me and stopped within an inch of my face, a fist raised. "Don't you dare start spreading rumors about me or I'll have you –" Spittle flew from his mouth.

I stepped back casually. "Such a lot of anger. Maybe enough to kill."

His nostrils flared. Then he took a deep breath and made a show of straightening his jacket.

"I've worked hard in this town. People trust me, and you shouldn't be here trying to turn everything upside down. Now leave me alone." He stormed back toward the door and banged through it. It slammed shut, the sound echoing like a gunshot in the small church.

*Why doesn't he want me asking questions?* I thought to myself as I walked outside. *What is he hiding?*

# CHAPTER TWENTY-FOUR

I sat in the 4-Runner for a moment, blasted the air-conditioner, and called Cal. I wanted him to check into Toby Holder's finances, and do a quick background check on Sheehan to see if either one was hiding something. He didn't answer, so I left a message for him to call me, and then spent the next half-hour trying to find Toby Holder.

I drove back to Holder Farm Equipment, but it was closed for the evening, and no one was around. That meant Toby might've gone home. I paid his house another visit, this time with no illegal intent. He didn't answer, so I cruised through town, hoping to see him somewhere. I didn't, but a thought occurred to me. Everyone in Sagebrush seemed to feel a need to put on airs with Pastor Sheehan. Maybe Toby would show up for services later that night. If so, I could be there to talk to him.

I stopped at the café for a bite to eat, where, by the way, I was becoming one of the "regulars," then made it to the church with a few minutes to spare. The parking lot was full, as was the church. I slipped into a row in the back just as a man with a guitar led the congregation in a hymn. I stood up and sang as I searched the crowd for Toby. He wasn't there, but Mayor Holder was in the front row, along with Annette Gessler and her husband.

I waited, hoping Toby would show up. The congregation sang a few more songs, and ten minutes later, we sat down, but still no Toby. Thinking I was wasting my time – at least from the standpoint of finding Toby – I was starting to slip out of the pew when Pastor Sheehan's voice boomed throughout the small church.

"A stranger in our midst."

I quietly sat back down and looked toward him. He was staring at me.

"My sermon tonight is about leaving the past behind."

*So what was the bit about a stranger?* I thought.

I held Sheehan's gaze and decided to stay as he continued his sermon. He talked about not dredging up things from the past, and how to ask for forgiveness for things one has done long ago. Was that specifically for certain members of his flock?

As he spoke, he kept glancing nervously at me. *If he was hiding something from his own past, let him worry about this investigator in his present*, I thought. I was going to find Marcia, and if it meant digging up something from 1985, so be it.

Sheehan droned on, and the service finally concluded with another hymn. As everyone stood up, Holder went to Sheehan and they had a brief conversation. Both made eye contact with me. Mayor Holder frowned, then gestured at Sheehan and they disappeared through the door near the altar.

*I've got them nervous*, I thought. I just wished I knew about what.

I waited a moment, then moseyed outside. Night had fallen. I got in the 4-Runner, not sure what to do next. Then Bogie spoke and I grabbed my phone.

"You rang?" Cal said.

"Lower your voice a bit and you'd sound like Lurch from *The*

*Addams Family*."

He laughed, but quickly grew serious. "I did a check on John Smith."

"And?"

"The guy apparently came into existence in 1985. I couldn't find anything on him before that. No birth records, schooling records, no tax returns or other documentation before that."

"Like he created a new identity at that time."

"Right," he said.

"Anything odd in his background since 1985?"

"No, nothing unusual. He's worked as an accountant, doesn't cheat on his taxes – if anything he pays more than he should – and there's nothing to make anyone suspicious of him."

"Like someone who's trying to fly under the radar."

"Exactly. I checked his phone records, too, and there aren't any calls to Marcia Holder or anyone in Sagebrush, either."

"Okay, thanks. Can you run a quick check for me now on Toby Holder and Franklin Sheehan? Check their finances, and see if either one has a record."

I heard him typing. "Spell Sheehan."

I did, and he hummed while he worked. "Give me a few minutes, okay?"

"Sure."

"I'll call you back."

Then he was gone.

It had been a long day, and I was ready to go back to the hotel. I took a meandering drive through town and once again passed by Holder Farm Equipment. Dim light came from the front of the store, probably a light or two left on to deter burglars. I turned the corner and noticed that a light was coming from a back office window. Typical to leave a light on in the back as well?

Curious, I did a U-turn, parked across the street, and got out. It was quiet, no sound of traffic, people, dogs, or anything else. I was about to cross the street when my cell phone rang. I swore, yanked it from my pocket, and cut Bogie off before he could complete his line.

"Hey," I said to Cal as I hopped back in the 4-Runner.

"You sound flustered."

"I forgot to silence my phone," I said. "And it's eerily silent a-round this town."

He ignored that and said, "Okay, nothing spectacular about Shee-han. He's married, two grown kids, and has lived in Sagebrush since 1968. He doesn't have a record, and his finances are in order. He bought his house in '75, and he just paid it off. Nothing unusual with his bank-ing, either. The guy looks clean."

"What about Toby Holder?"

"He had a few arrests right after high school, but nothing since. He's never married, makes a decent living with Holder Farm Equipment, and his taxes are in order."

"What about his house? Is it paid for?"

"Yes. He's got the house and twenty acres."

I whistled. "It's a really nice place." I described it for him. "He's paying big bucks for his liquor and cigar selection, and he's got some expensive cars, too. Would the trust pay for that?"

"No, he invests that money."

"Then his store is making enough for his high living?"

"Tsk, tsk. I don't think so. On paper, he's not rich. Holder Farm

Equipment does pretty well, but he's got expenses with it that keep him from clearing a fortune."

"Where's he getting the money for his man cave and other toys?"

"You're the detective."

"Funny," I said.

He laughed. "Hey, I've got some other work to do, but I'll keep monitoring John Smith's calls for you."

"Thanks, I appreciate it."

"What're you going to do next?"

I gazed at the square of light coming from the office window. "I'm going to see if I can talk to Toby. He's not on the level."

"Good luck," he said and ended the call.

I silenced the phone, pocketed it, slid back out of the car, and ran across the street. I crept along the side of the building toward the window where the light was on. As I neared it, I realized the window was open. Country music filtered out. I pressed myself against the wall and listened. No voices, only the music.

I edged forward and peeked inside.

The office was large, with high ceilings, white walls, file cabinets, and a metal desk that faced the door to the main part of the store. Toby was at the desk, typing at his computer. Then he sat back, grabbed a cell phone off the desk and started talking to someone. I strained to hear over the music. He said something about 'coming soon,' and he was ready. He talked for a few minutes more, shook his head, and glanced at a big clock on the wall that read 9:30. Then he shrugged, and said something else. With a final wave of his hand, he ended the call and set the phone back on the desk. At that moment, I stood in front of the window and rapped on the glass.

He pushed himself out of the chair, saying, "You're early, and why the hell aren't you coming around front?" Then he turned and saw me. His jaw dropped, but he quickly recovered. "What're you doing here?" he snarled.

"You're a hard man to find," I said as I rested my forearms on the window ledge.

"Get out of here!"

"You're up to something," I said. "Marcia knew about it, right? And you've done something to her."

"How dare you think I would harm my sister! I was there for her!"

He stepped around the desk and grabbed a pistol lying beside the computer. I hadn't seen the weapon. I held up my hands.

"I don't want any problems," I said. I stepped away from the window. "I just want to know where Marcia is."

"I don't know." He reached the window and aimed at me. "Get out of here and don't come back."

I didn't break his gaze as I backpedaled and made my way across the street to the 4-Runner. I revved the engine and squealed off down the street, but I wasn't leaving. Toby was expecting someone, and I wanted to know who. So I drove around the corner and parked. Then I took out my Glock, put it in the small of my back, grabbed binoculars from the backseat, and sneaked back to the corner. I hid behind a big evergreen in an empty lot, where I could see the front of Holder Farm Equipment and the side of the building near the street. Toby was still silhouetted in the window. He waited a long time before finally moving away.

I hunkered down and watched the building. Stars came out, but the light stayed on in Toby's office. Eleven o'clock came and went, and Toby never left. It grew chilly and I wished I had thought to bring a light jacket. Midnight arrived. I yawned, shifted, but didn't leave. I wanted to know what Toby was up to, and I wasn't going anywhere until I knew. Finally, at close to one, a large flatbed truck rumbled down the street. It pulled into the front of Holder Farm Equipment. Toby opened a gate to the back lot and the truck drove though. The engine died, and an eerie silence filled the air.

I couldn't see the truck anymore, so I ducked down and ran across the street. I lay down in some tall weeds near the perimeter fence and trained my binoculars into the back lot.

Two men got out of the truck cab, and they worked with Toby to unload some farm equipment into a garage bay. When they finished, one of the men bent down and pulled something from under the wheel well of a riding lawn mower. I'd seen something like that before. Through the binoculars, it appeared to be a brick of marijuana, or possibly heroin. Toby whacked the guy on the head with the palm of his hand, then gestured at the other man to close the garage door. He did, and I wasn't able to see anything more.

I stared up at the fence. It was at least ten feet high. I wondered if I could quietly scale it and get into the lot. I reached out and grabbed the chain link. It rattled loudly. Then I heard a dog bark somewhere down the street. What if he kept barking and someone else was in the lot and heard the ruckus? I didn't want to risk it. Besides, there were no windows for me to look in anyway. I decided to wait and see what happened next.

Time crept by. I was growing tired, and I stifled another yawn. The weeds were making me itch, and I scratched my eyes. Finally, the garage door opened. The two men got back in the truck. I ducked down as the headlights cut a path through the lot. Then the truck hit the street and rumbled away. A minute later, Toby came out, shut the garage door, and went to a silver truck parked near the gate. He drove out the gate, stopped long enough to shut and lock it, then hit the street. I pressed myself into the ground as the truck passed by. I waited until I couldn't hear the engine, then slowly rose to my feet. I wished I could get into the store, but I suspected there would be an alarm system. And I had what I needed to know. Toby Holder appeared to be smuggling drugs. I had something I could take to the sheriff in the morning.

I ran back to the 4-Runner, brushed myself off, and got in. I was shivering as I drove back to the hotel. I grabbed my backpack and trudged inside. The night clerk barely noticed me as I walked down the hall to my room. I put the key in and unlocked the door, stepped into the room and froze. Someone was there. I gently set the backpack down, pulled out my Glock, aimed into the room, and flipped the light switch on.

Lying on the bed, with the covers partially thrown back, was Willie in a sexy black teddy. She suddenly sat up and blinked.

"Geez!" I said as I lowered the Glock. "What're you doing here?"

"I was missing you, so I found someone to cover my shift. I drove up to surprise you." She yawned and stretched.

My eyes roved up and down her body. "I'm surprised," I said.

"I got a key from the desk clerk – he recognized me from our last visit – and waited for you to come back. Then I, uh … fell asleep. Why're you so late?"

I shrugged as I put the Glock in my backpack and put it near the bed. Then, after my heartrate slowed down, I eyed her again.

"What?" she said.

"You're by far the best thing I've seen all day."

She twirled her hair in her hand. "Want to come to bed?"

I nodded. "I do."

# CHAPTER TWENTY-FIVE

The next morning, I slept later than I meant to. Willie and I had breakfast at the hotel, and then she was going to spend a little time at the pool, and then study for some continuing education classes she needed to take. While she did that, I visited the sheriff. It was almost ten when I parked in front of a long, red brick building a block from Main Street. A blue Tahoe was sitting near the door, but no car sat in the slot reserved for the sheriff.

I strolled through double-glass doors and into a small lobby that smelled faintly of Clorox. A woman in a tan uniform sat at a desk near the door, gazing at a monitor on her desk. Behind her were two doors and two windows covered with partially closed blinds. The woman looked up and gave me a warm smile.

"Something I can do for you?"

"Is Sheriff Madisen here?" I asked.

"He's not here right now. Can I help you?"

I glanced around. "No, I'll try later." I went back outside before she could ask me any questions.

I drove around town for a while, then went by Holder Farm Equipment. Toby's silver truck sat near the gate. I parked down the street, where I could see into the back lot. I watched through my binoculars for a while, but never saw Toby or the men I'd seen with him the previous night. Some of the farm equipment that had been delivered last night was sitting near the building, but nothing that would indicate drug smuggling. Toby Holder wasn't that stupid. When my stomach growled, I finally left, got a late lunch with Willie, and then tried to find Sheriff Madisen. I called the sheriff's department and left a message, asking for him to call me. Then I resumed my watch of Holder Farm Equipment. Finally, around four, the sheriff called me back.

"I understand you want to talk to me?" he said.

"Yes, I –"

"My office. Be here in ten minutes."

» » » » »

"Good timing on your part," the deputy said when I entered the sheriff's department. "The sheriff is here. May I tell him your name?"

Just then, the door to the right opened and Sheriff Ben Madisen poked his head out.

"Come on in," he said in a deep voice.

The woman nodded, and Madisen waved a hand at me. I crossed the lobby and went into his office. He shut the door behind me.

"Have a seat." He gestured at a black barrel chair in front of a large desk.

I took a seat as he settled into a leather office chair. His office was dim, with dark paneled walls, dark green carpet, and little in the way of lighting. On the wall behind him, shelves displayed awards, and pictures of him with the mayor, other officers, and even the governor.

Sheriff Madisen was wearing a baseball cap with the sheriff's logo on it. He adjusted the cap, then steepled his fingers and gazed at me. "I hear you're running around town asking a lot of questions."

I held up my hands. "And someone doesn't like it."

"Why do you say that?"

"A car ran me off the road the other night. I almost went through a barbed wire fence and into a field."

"Did you get a license plate number?"

I shook my head.

"Did you see the driver?"

"No."

He pursed his lips. "I can file a report if you want, but it seems kind of pointless."

"Not necessary."

He studied me, then said, "What do you need?"

I stared back at him. "How much do you know about Toby Holder?"

He chose his words carefully. "He's a good man, represents this community well. Everyone likes him. And he's my brother-in-law, so I know him a bit better than most. Why?"

"I have reason to suspect he's smuggling drugs."

His face remained impassive. Then he unfolded his hands and leaned forward, elbows on the desk. "That's a serious allegation you're making."

"I know."

"Is that the real reason why you've come to Sagebrush? You're investigating Toby Holder?"

"No. I want to find Marcia Holder. That's why I wanted to talk to your wife."

He snorted. "If she doesn't want to talk to you, I certainly wouldn't be able to change that."

202                                Renée Pawlish

"Has she heard from Marcia recently?"

"Not that I'm aware of."

I pointed at him. "And *you* haven't?"

"No."

"Okay," I said. "In the course of my inquiries, I discovered that Toby Holder leads a pretty extravagant lifestyle, one that needs more money than he's making at Holder Farm Equipment."

"How did you find all this out?"

"I can't reveal," I said.

He leaned back. "I'm going to need more than that."

"Last night at one a.m., a truck delivered some farm equipment to Toby's store. That itself seemed odd, but I also saw one of the truck drivers pull something out from the wheel well of a riding lawn mower and hand it to Toby."

"So?"

"It appeared to be a brick of marijuana, or possibly heroin."

He rubbed his chin, then said, "Are you sure it was drugs?"

"Pretty sure."

"What were you doing out there at that time of night?"

I shrugged. "Detecting."

He didn't laugh at that. "Did anyone else see them?"

"I don't know. I would assume I was the only one."

"Do you have any other proof of possible drug smuggling?"

"No."

He thought again. "No pictures or video of this transaction, or any other?"

"No," I repeated.

"Hmm." He steepled the hands again. "What if you're wrong?"

"Isn't it worth checking? Toby used to be friends with a man named Jay Overstrom. Overstrom was shot and killed execution-style, and it was thought that he associated with drug smugglers in Denver."

"Yes, I'm familiar with the case. It was never solved."

"Toby was friends with Overstrom. What if Toby's continued the smuggling operation?"

"Without me knowing?"

"He's the son of the longtime mayor." I hesitated. "If he's careful about what he does, why would anyone suspect him? I also think your father-in-law and Pastor Sheehan are hiding something. What if they know about what Toby's doing, or what if they're involved?"

"What makes you think either are involved?"

I told him what I'd unearthed in my investigation.

"You're accusing three of the top people in this town of some very serious crimes."

"I may be wrong, but it's at least worth checking."

He pondered that. "I hate to accuse Toby of something like this if it isn't true."

He didn't want to think what I said might be valid. Maybe he had been letting things slip past his "watchful" eye and didn't want to admit it.

"There's something I can't figure out," I said.

"Oh? What's that?"

"How Marcia Holder is involved in this."

He cocked an eyebrow at me. "You think she's involved in smuggling drugs?"

"I don't think so, but why did she disappear right after I found her?" I told him about how I'd been hired to find her, and the scene at her house, with the broken lamp and the blood, and how she showed up at her father's house the previous night.

"Marcia went to his house?"

I nodded. "You hadn't heard that?"

He shook his head.

"Did you know he was paying for her to live in Denver?"

"No," he said. "I thought she'd run away. All these years, she was that close." He stared past me, then whispered, "The old man never said anything."

"I get the feeling Mayor Holder doesn't want anyone to know." I hesitated again. "His kids don't like him."

He ignored that. "You think someone tried to hurt Marcia the other night in Denver?" he asked.

"I'd lean that way. There was a fight, she escaped, then came up here to find out why someone's coming for her after all these years. What if she knew that Toby was a drug smuggler?"

"Why would she keep her mouth shut all this time?"

I grimaced. "Maybe since he's her brother. But when I talked to her, I got the feeling she had something on her father, and the deal was if he paid her bills, she'd keep her mouth shut about him. And *he* told me himself that when she talked to him the other night, she said she was here because of something from the past. What was that about?"

He threw up a hand. "How should I know?" He stared hard at me. "I can't speak to what Marcia might be thinking or doing now, but I do know that what she did back in '85 was very hurtful to her whole family."

"From what I've heard, it was more about Mayor Holder being embarrassed, and him and Pastor Sheehan worrying about her pregnancy reflecting poorly on them."

"I don't know about that, but she shouldn't have gotten herself into that situation in the first place."

"What about the guy? He had a piece in that."

He didn't respond.

"And you know about how Mayor Holder dragged her back from Kansas?" I asked.

He nodded. "That was awful. Everyone was upset that she'd left, and then to have a big fight like that, and Marcia getting knocked around and hitting her head."

"Who told you that?"

"Jennifer. She heard it from Marcia."

I mulled that over. Marcia had thought she'd fallen and hit her head. Did Jennifer know what really happened at the hotel? Had she been talking to John Smith? I made a mental note to ask Smith about that – and Jennifer, if she'd talk to me again.

"Jennifer didn't hear that from someone else?" I danced carefully, not wanting to let the sheriff know I thought his wife might be lying.

His eyes narrowed. "Like who?"

"Did she talk to the guy Marcia had been dating?"

"Impossible. None of us knew who Marcia had been seeing." He suddenly stood up. "I have some other things to attend to, but I'll look into this situation with Toby. I appreciate you letting me know. We don't want any trouble in this town."

I'd offended him. I got up as well. "Thanks for your time."

"You're staying at the Sagebrush Inn?"

"Yes."

"Good. If I need anything from you, I'll go there."

"Will you at least talk to Toby and let me know if I'm wrong?"

"I suppose I can do that."

I wasn't convinced he was going to do anything. It seemed like I'd have to supply him with more evidence before he'd act. But how?

He waved a dismissive hand at me, and was already picking up the phone when I left his office.

# CHAPTER TWENTY-SIX

I drove to the end of the block, where I could still see Madisen's cruiser in the parking lot. He hadn't seemed convinced that Toby Holder might be doing something illegal, and I wanted to know what Madisen would do next. I shut off the 4-Runner, rolled down my window, and grabbed a pad and pen from the glove compartment. Then I pulled out my phone and called Gina Smith. She picked up immediately.

"I need your father's phone number," I said as I kept my eye on the sheriff's department. "I've got to ask him some questions."

"He's not around and he isn't returning my calls."

"Since when?"

"Since you met with him."

"When's the last time you called him?"

"Last night." She sighed. "After you two talked at his house the night before, he was so upset."

"Yeah, I remember."

"Well, he called me yesterday and said he was going out of town for a few days, and he couldn't watch Ethan. When I asked him where he was going, he wouldn't say, just that he had some things to take care of, and not to worry. But he sounded worried. Do you think something's happened to him, too?"

I bit my lip. "It doesn't look good. Give me his number and I'll see if he'll answer for me."

She rattled it off and I wrote it down. "If he answers, I'll let you know."

"Thanks," she said. "Reed, what's going on?"

I gazed down the block. "I'm not sure, but I'm close to something. I'll keep you posted. Oh, what kind of car does your father drive?"

"A Mazda sedan. Why?"

"Is it dark, with four doors?"

"Yes, why?"

I didn't answer directly. "I'll keep an eye out for him, in case he's in Sagebrush."

"Okay."

I ended the call, then dialed John Smith's number. It rang four times and went to voice mail. I wasn't surprised. I left a message, saying it was urgent that he call me back as soon as possible, but I didn't have high hopes that he would.

I sat for a minute as questions circled in my brain. I hadn't trusted John Smith from the start. Was he hiding something, and had he come to Sagebrush, and was *he* the one who tried to run me off the road the other night? I glanced around. Where was he now?

My next call was to Jennifer Madisen. As expected, it went to voice mail. I asked her to call me as well, again not expecting her to do so. I jammed my phone back in my pocket, frustrated. How could I make sense of this mess if no one would talk to me? I didn't have time to think about that, because just then Sheriff Madisen walked out of the building and stomped to his cruiser, then drove off down the street. I waited until he'd turned the corner and then I followed.

The cruiser went to Main Street, but instead of turning right as I would've expected if Madisen was going to Holder Farm Equipment, it went left. Where was he going? I didn't have to wait long for my answer. The cruiser drove slowly along Main Street, then pulled in by the park.

Madisen got out and casually leaned against the hood. I whipped down a side street and parked, then hopped out. I ran to the corner of a building and peeked around it, my eye on Sheriff Madisen. A moment later, Mayor Holder strolled out of the park and up to his son-in-law. The two spoke for a few minutes, and then Holder waved and walked to his Cadillac. He slid behind the wheel and started in my direction. Madisen got into his cruiser and drove the other way.

I dashed back to the 4-Runner, ducked down as Holder's Cadillac passed by, then pulled onto Main Street. The cruiser was two blocks ahead of me. I stayed with it, still expecting Madisen to turn and head for Holder Farm Equipment. But he didn't. The cruiser reached the end of Main and turned onto the highway. I sped up, but by the time I got onto the highway, Madisen was almost out of view. He soon turned onto County Road 15.

*He's headed home for the night*, I thought.

Had he even talked to Toby Holder? And why had he needed to talk to Mayor Holder? To alert him about Toby?

I reached County Road 15, but instead of following Madisen, I turned around and headed back into town. I seemed to be at a dead end. I shrugged and called Willie.

"Want to join me for a bite to eat?"

"You can take a break from your investigation?"

I sighed. "It seems so. I can pick you up in ten minutes."

"I'll be ready."

"Great." Maybe dinner with my wife would lighten my mood.

» » » » »

Willie and I decided to mix it up, and we had a decent dinner at an Italian restaurant a few blocks down from the café. While we ate, I caught her up on my day. She had a sexy tan and was relaxed. I wished I could say the same for myself.

"You'll figure it out," she was saying when I held up my hand to interrupt her. "What?"

"There's Jennifer Madisen," I said as I saw Jennifer pass by the front window of the restaurant. "Hold on."

I scooted out of the restaurant and ran after Jennifer.

"Hey!" I called out.

She glanced over her shoulder, realized it was me, and said, "Leave me alone."

"I just want to know if you knew who Marcia had been dating, the guy who got her pregnant."

She rolled her eyes. "No."

"Your husband –"

"We didn't know anything. Now leave me alone!" she repeated and stormed off down the street.

I was standing there, wondering if she was telling the truth, when Willie came outside.

"I paid for dinner."

"Huh? Oh, thanks." I kissed her. "Sorry. Let's go back to the hotel."

"Sounds good."

We were headed there when Cal called. "You're never going to believe this."

"What?"

"John Smith received a couple of interesting calls today."

I didn't like his tone. "One was from me, but who else?"

"There was a call earlier today from a 970 area code."

"Let me guess, the 970 is from Mayor Holder."

"Close. Toby Holder called him."

I gripped the phone harder. "Toby's been lying to me this whole time."

"It looks like it."

"If Toby knows Smith, does Jennifer or the mayor know him as well?" I mused. "And Smith didn't receive any calls from Mayor Holder or anyone else from Sagebrush?"

"No, just that one."

"Okay, thanks."

"What's going on?"

I quickly filled him in. When I finished, he said, "You watch your back. If Toby's involved with some kind of drug cartel, these guys will shoot you dead without any reason."

"I will." I put the phone away and glanced at Willie. "I need to run you back to the hotel, and then I need to find Toby Holder."

"I can go with you."

I started to protest, but she shook her head. "Come on, Reed, let me go with you. If I wait at the hotel, I'll just worry about you. This way, I can stay in the car, but if something happens, I can get help."

"What's going to happen?"

She looked at me askance. "Trouble always finds you."

"Ouch," I said. "Fine. But I'm sure you'll be bored."

She shrugged. "I've helped you before and it's been kind of fun."

I saw the look on her face, and I didn't think I'd win this argument, so I didn't protest further. "Are we becoming the new Nick and Nora Charles from *The Thin Man*?" I said, referring to Dashiell Hammett's 1930s detective duo.

She laughed. "Could be. Except that you're not a hard-drinking ex-detective, and I'm not a wealthy socialite."

I smiled at her. "You've watched the movies."

"A couple of them."

I shook my head, ever in awe of my wife.

"Let's check Toby's store again, and if he isn't there, we'll go back to the hotel," I said.

"Fine."

I whipped a U-turn and headed for Holder Farm Equipment. Dusk was settling in as I neared the store, and then I saw Toby's silver truck sitting out front.

I pointed at it. "He's there."

"The store's dark," Willie said. "So where is he?"

"Maybe in back."

I went by the parking lot, turned the corner, and passed by his office. The window was closed, and no light was coming from inside. Where was Holder? I drove around the back of the building.

"There's a rear entrance," Willie said.

"It leads to Eleventh Street," I observed.

I went back around the block and ended up in front of the store. I parked on the street, near the closed gate to the back lot, and got out.

"Go around to the side of the building again," I said. "If you see the office light come on, or if Holder goes out the back door, call and let me know."

She nodded, slid across to the driver's seat, and drove off. I set my phone to vibrate, then walked along the fence and around to the front parking lot. The store was quiet. I stood near the chain link fence and watched the front door for a minute to see if I could spot Toby Holder inside.

Nothing.

I was moving toward the door when a loud crack echoed into the air. It had come from somewhere in the back lot. I knelt down, unholstered my Glock, and peered through the fence. I let my eyes rove around. The lot was full of farm equipment and shadows. Then I spied movement off to the left.

I grabbed the fence and, as quickly and as quietly as possible, climbed it. It still rattled loudly. I dropped down on the other side and listened. I sneaked past some kind of big tractor with a rotating blade on the front – I'm a city boy, so I don't know what it is – and saw someone rush past a big green cart with big wheels near the rear of the lot. I ducked down and dashed between rows of equipment. Somewhere ahead of me, I heard footsteps. I moved forward cautiously. A huge light on the side of the building came on, illuminating the lot in silver brightness, but also creating pale shadows. As I neared a big John Deere tractor, another crack rang out and a rush of air whizzed by my face. He'd shot at me! I flattened onto the ground, my heart pounding. That was too close for comfort.

After ten seconds, I pushed into a crouch. Then I saw a form running toward the building. I aimed the Glock, but he was gone. I looked all around, and listened. Where was he?

Then, over the sounds of my breathing, I heard a groan. I squatted down and moved to the end of the tractor. The groan came again. I peeked around the tractor and in the dim light saw John Smith. He was propped against the huge tire of the tractor. He had on jeans and a white T-shirt, but the shirt had a growing stain on it.

## CHAPTER TWENTY-SEVEN

I swore, then dropped to my knees. I shoved the Glock in the small of my back as I stared at Smith. He'd been shot in the gut. He had one hand covering the wound, but blood oozed between his fingers.

"Did Toby shoot you?" I asked.

He nodded. He was breathing in short gasps. I heard a truck engine rev to life, and then my phone vibrated. It was Willie.

"Toby Holder's leaving," she said in a soft voice.

"I know. He shot John Smith."

"What? No!"

"You've got to come back here. Can you climb the fence?"

"Yes. Where are you?"

I looked around. "In the back corner."

"I'm on my way."

I ended the call, then stared at Smith. "Hold tight, and keep your hand on the wound. My wife is a nurse, and she can help. And I'm calling 911."

I punched 911 into the phone.

He reached out and grabbed my arm and whispered, "It's too late."

"What?"

He shook his head. "You need to protect Marcia."

"What?" I said. The operator came on the line, and I told her a man had been shot, and where I was. She said she'd send an ambulance and the police. She started to ask more questions.

"Hold on," I said to her, then held the phone away from my ear so I could hear Smith.

I glanced around, then looked back at Smith. "Is Marcia here?"

"She went after him. But he'll kill her."

"Who?"

The operator said something and I put the phone to my ear. She was asking more questions, but I needed to hear Smith.

"Just send someone, and hurry," I said, then disconnected.

Smith took in a few gasps. A faint odor of engine grease mixed with the metallic smell of blood. He gestured at me to listen to him. "I was involved with the drugs."

"Now?"

He shook his head again. "Back then. When I was working at the dairy plant. Another guy and I worked with some locals, bringing drugs up from Mexico."

"Jay Overstrom."

He nodded. "When Marcia got pregnant, I knew I wanted out. I … didn't want her and the baby involved with any of that. I loved her. Still do. But they found us at the hotel in Russell."

"Who did?"

He seemed to find a reserve of strength. "They killed Jay because he was getting careless. Then his wife started asking too many questions, so they were going to get rid of her, too. I knew the plan, didn't want any part of it, but I knew what was going on, so they didn't want me around, either."

"Who's they, and why didn't they kill you in Kansas?"

"I escaped. Came back for Marcia later."

"Did she know about the drug smuggling?"

"No. She knew I had a past. When we left, I told her I was going straight. She was young, naïve. So much potential. We loved each other."

"Reed!" I heard Willie call out in a low voice.

"Over here!" I hissed.

Smith's face scrunched up.

"It's okay," I said. "It's my wife."

Willie rushed around the front of the tractor. In one hand she held a spare towel that she'd grabbed from the backseat of the 4-Runner. She took in the scene, then hurried over and sank to her knees by us.

"Let me look." She started to touch Smith, but he pushed her hands away. "Please," she whispered.

"Too late," he said.

He was struggling to speak, but there was clear urgency in his voice. Willie again tried to examine the gunshot wound, and he again pushed her away. She was able to press the towel to the wound, and she held it there.

"Let me talk," he said forcefully.

She leaned back, frustration crossing her face, but let him speak. Smith looked at me.

"How did they find Marcia now, in Denver?" I asked.

"My fault." He took a few short breaths. "When I saw the news ... the remains being found in the field near Woodrow, I panicked. That was where they put Jay's wife. They were supposed to hide the body where it would never be found." He sucked in a breath. "Only person I'd ever told about all this was my friend, Greg Martinez. I called him about the body, and Gina overheard me." He scowled. "Wish she hadn't." He breathed heavily for a moment. "Greg told me I should go to the police, clean the slate. At first, I didn't want to … I'd go to jail. But he was right. It's time to come clean. I'm tired of the guilt. I screwed up. I called Toby to tell him what I was going to do. That it was over." He grimaced. "Never should've done that. Now they think Marcia knows, too."

My jaw dropped. "Is Toby after his own sister?"

He shook his head. "He protected her."

"From who?"

Sadness crossed his face. "She couldn't remember what happened in Russell. She wasn't a threat."

"Marcia?" I asked.

It was getting harder for him to talk, and he seemed to be going in and out of consciousness. "But he doesn't believe her."

"Tell me who!" I couldn't follow what he was saying.

"He wants her dead. Toby told me. I came up here to stop them. I confronted Toby first. Thought I could get him to reason. He went crazy. I ran and he shot me." He took a deep, gargled breath. "Should've told you Mayor Holder wasn't involved, but was afraid of what you'd find out. Didn't want you to know about the smuggling. I knew it would put Marcia and Gina in danger."

He groaned, and then wheezed.

"Where is the ambulance?" I muttered. I was losing him. "Did you tell Jennifer or anyone else what happened in that hotel room?" I asked quickly.

"No," he whispered. "No one was there but us. I didn't tell any-body. Marcia didn't even remember, and I never told her."

"What's your real name?"

He managed a faint smile. "Doesn't matter now. I don't have any family except Gina."

He sucked in one final short breath and let it out in a gurgle. Then his eyes glazed over, and his body went limp. I sat back on my haunches while Willie took his pulse.

"He's dead," she murmured.

I slowly nodded.

"Why wouldn't he let us try to help?" she asked.

I shrugged. "I don't think he would've survived, and I'm not sure he wanted to."

She gazed down at him. "What was he talking about?"

I didn't answer, instead mentally going over what Smith had just said. I had bits and pieces of a story that I was trying to fit together with everything else I'd learned.

"Where is the ambulance?" Willie said.

I hardly heard her, my mind racing. Willie looked at me.

"I can tell by the look on your face that you've figured out something, but I'm confused."

"I've been focused on the wrong things," I said. "This small town," I waved a hand around, "and all the weirdness…"

"Reed, what is it?" she asked.

I suddenly had the last piece of the puzzle.

# CHAPTER TWENTY-EIGHT

"The other Madisen was lying to me," I said, mostly to myself.

Her brow furrowed. "What?"

"I thought Jennifer Madisen was lying to me." I gestured at Smith's body. "If what he said is true, and he didn't tell Marcia what happened in that hotel room, then how could Jennifer have known?"

She shrugged. "I'm not following."

"Sheriff Madisen said he knew about the fight in the hotel room in Kansas because Jennifer told him about it. And *she* knew because Marcia told her," I said. "But Marcia didn't remember about the fight, and Smith never told her, or anyone else, about it. If all that's true, that means either Sheriff Madisen – who's Marcia's brother-in-law – was in that hotel room, or Toby Holder, her own brother, was there and told him."

"Madisen was involved with Toby Holder in drug smuggling?"

"It sure looks that way."

I growled, and then swore. Earlier today I'd told Madisen all my suspicions of Toby Holder, and Madisen was involved in the whole thing.

"What?" Willie said.

I waved a hand in frustration. "Never mind."

Sirens sounded in the distance and quickly drew closer. Fast reaction in a small town. In seconds the sirens wailed close by, and we heard vehicles screech to a stop. I moved to the end of the tractor and peered around it. An ambulance and a sheriff's car were in the parking lot, lights flashing. A man got out of the car and started toward the fence. He crossed under a streetlight and I saw that it was not Sheriff Madisen.

I grabbed Willie's arm. "I've got to find Madisen and Toby Holder. But if I stay here, I could be tied up all night with questions, so you talk to the deputy. Tell them who you are and what happened, and that I've gone out to Sheriff Madisen's house because I think something's going on out there."

"Don't you want to tell the deputy what you suspect?"

I shook my head. "There's no time. And I don't have any proof just yet, and then Madisen would know I'm onto him. He's got everyone in this town fooled. Just tell them to send someone out to his house, and I'll take it from there."

"Oh!" She held up a hand. "What if the deputy's involved?"

"If he is, he's not going to do anything with the paramedics right here."

"Okay, I'll handle it."

"Where are the car keys?"

She handed them to me. "I'll see if the deputy can give me a ride back to the hotel. Or I'll walk. It's not that far."

I stood up and helped her to her feet. "Go tell them what's going on, but raise your hands and be careful."

"I can handle it," she repeated.

I kissed her hard. "I love you. I'll check on you in a few minutes." I squeezed her hand, then ran to the back of the lot. I climbed the fence, worried that the deputy would hear the sound I was making. I dropped down on the other side, then crouched down and listened. Willie called out, and the deputy replied, but I couldn't understand what he said. I sneaked along to the end of the fence and listened again, then stole up to the back side of the building and peered around the corner. The 4-Runner was sitting in the dark, with no one around it. I hurried down the street to it, quietly eased inside and started it. I swung a U-turn and crawled down the street, but waited until I turned the corner before I flipped on the headlights. Then I glanced in the rearview mirror. No one was following me. I finally breathed a little easier.

A few minutes later, I passed by the sheriff's department. The building was quiet, and Sheriff Madisen's parking space was empty. He wasn't there, so I headed out of town. Partway there I called Willie.

"Everything okay?"

"They're dealing with Smith now," she said. "I tried to tell the deputy that you're heading out to Madisen's ranch because you think there might be trouble out there, and he looked at me like I'm crazy. Then he said he'd get to me in a few minutes."

"It's okay. Just do what they say, and tell them when you can."

"I will."

I ended the call, and in fifteen minutes, I neared the Madisen ranch. I shut off my headlights, drove a little farther and parked behind a grove of trees near the road, then took out my binoculars. A single light was on in a front window, but no cars were parked in front of the garage. None of that told me whether Sheriff Madisen or Jennifer was home. A weak light above the garage bathed the front of the house in shadows, but the road was dark.

I got out, then walked down the road. I climbed the porch steps and listened. I couldn't hear voices, a TV, or any other noises coming from the house. I rang the bell and waited.

Silence.

I tried the knob, and as expected, it turned. I let myself in and strained to hear anything while I let my eyes adjust. Then I looked around. I was standing in a huge foyer with a tile floor and antique armoire near the door. A lamp was on in a large living room to the left of the foyer, but the house was so big, the light from the lamp barely dented the darkness.

I tiptoed into the living room and glanced around. A large window looked out onto the front porch. I listened, but still heard nothing, so I stole across to a dining area and huge kitchen. But Sheriff Madisen and Jennifer weren't around, and neither was Marcia.

The house was massive, and it took me a long time to make my way through the rest of the rooms on the main floor. There were several bedrooms upstairs that I checked – all empty – and then I found the stairs to the basement. Sheriff Madisen had a man cave every bit as big and expensive as Toby Holder's, and a massive wine cellar full of what I assumed to be pricey bottles of wine. It would've taken more than a sheriff's salary and the measly trust fund to afford all of it.

I finally returned to the foyer and was about to check the garage when I heard a car come up the road. I froze. Headlights flashed by the front window and disappeared. I hurried over to the edge of the window and peeked out.

A sedan was pulling into the driveway, very similar to the one that had pushed me off the road. I shifted to the other side of the window where I could see the garage. The door opened, and the sedan pulled inside. The space next to it was empty. A moment later, Jennifer emerged from the car. Had she been following me the other night, or had it been the sheriff? I didn't have time to think that through because Jennifer was crossing the garage toward the house. If I didn't leave now, I'd be discovered.

I left the window and dashed through the dining area to the back door. I opened it and slipped out onto the patio. Just as I was closing the door, Jennifer entered the house. I ran across the porch and hid behind a large post. Lights came on in the kitchen and dining room. I peered around the post. Jennifer puttered around the kitchen, fixing a drink for herself. Then she moved off into the great room. Seconds later, lights came on in that room, and I heard voices. She'd turned on the TV.

I looked out toward the barn, and saw Sheriff Madisen's cruiser parked near the porch attached to the barn. Was he at the barn? I crouched down and slipped away from the house. The TV sounds faded away, and the night swallowed me. I stopped by the shed and waited, not relishing the thought of going to the barn. When I did, I'd be completely exposed.

I gathered up my courage and crept down the dark lane, stepping lightly in the soft dirt. It seemed to take forever to reach the barn. The corral was dark and empty. As I stole toward the fence, I thought I spotted movement on the far side of the building. I dropped to my knees, watched, and listened. A horse neighed, and then all was still and quiet again.

After a minute, I saw no one. Then I noticed a sliver of light coming from under the barn doors. I eased up to the fence, tiptoed along it to the side of the barn, then walked along the wall. I reached the far corner and peered around to the small porch on the back of the barn - the same porch where Jennifer had been enjoying her glass of lemonade the other day when I surprised her. Sheriff Madisen's cruiser was parked near the entrance to the barn. But from the house, I hadn't been able to see that Toby's silver truck was next to it. No one was on the porch, but a square of light from the window splashed on the floor.

I listened for a moment and thought I heard voices. I hopped over the porch railing and sneaked up to the window. I couldn't see anything, so I tiptoed toward the door. Then the voices became clearer.

Sheriff Madisen and Toby Holder were in the barn, and they were arguing loudly.

# CHAPTER TWENTY-NINE

"What the hell were you thinking?" Toby was saying. "I told you, Marcia doesn't remember anything about that night in Kansas, so she can't know that you were there. She doesn't know *anything* about the smuggling, so why the hell did you go to Denver? All you did was make her suspicious."

"I run this show," Sheriff Madisen replied. "With that private eye poking around, asking questions, he was going to figure things out."

"And you think killing my sister would've stopped that?"

"Shut up," Madisen said. "I'll handle that Ferguson guy."

"Like you did with Paula? She didn't stay buried, and Eddie saw it on the news. He called me."

*Eddie. That must be John Smith*, I thought.

"When?" Madisen sounded surprised.

"Yesterday. He said that he was tired of feeling guilty about what happened here, about Jay's death, and knowing what we'd done to Paula. He was going to go to the police to tell them everything."

I grabbed my Glock, held it in front of me, and peeked into the barn. Madisen was in uniform, but without his hat. He was standing near a stall, with his back to me. The tail of a large horse twitched behind him. Toby was facing Madisen, standing several feet away.

"Why didn't you tell me you talked to Eddie?" Madisen's voice was low and threatening.

"I was trying to take care of it because I knew you would go after him," Toby said angrily.

"You're right about that," Madisen snapped. "We should've killed him back in Russell, when we had the chance."

"It would've been taken care of, but you screwed that up." The sarcasm was clear in Toby's voice. "You should've tied him up better."

"And you shouldn't have been so worried about that damn baby crying." They didn't say anything for a moment, and then Madisen let out an audible sigh. "Well, Eddie's out of the picture now."

"Yeah, but what if that detective knows I shot him?"

"That's your problem."

"What're you talking about?"

Madisen laughed maliciously. "Simple. You're not leaving here."

"What?" Toby asked more forcefully.

"I'll say that you came out here to tell me what happened at your store, and when I told you I'd have to arrest you, you tried to go for my gun and I shot you."

Toby let out another string of curses, then said, "You're going to let me take the fall?"

"Of course."

Madisen reached for his gun, and I knew I had to act. I stood up and stepped into the barn, the Glock raised.

"Hold it right there," I said.

It was the cliché of clichés, but it worked. Madisen's hand stopped halfway to his holster. Toby's jaw dropped.

"It's the detective," Toby said.

"Raise your hands," I ordered.

Both men lifted their hands, and Madisen slowly turned around. I now noticed he had a cut on his forehead. I hadn't spotted it when I'd seen him before because he'd been wearing a hat.

"Get that from Marcia?" I asked, gesturing at his head.

Madisen stared at me for a second, then gave me an oily smile. "She was surprised when I showed up at her house in Denver, and stupid enough to let me in. But when I tried to grab her, she hit me with the lamp." He gingerly touched the cut. "The little tramp knocked me out. When I woke up, she was gone."

"And you came running back here with your tail between your legs," Toby said.

Madisen's eyebrows furrowed and his face turned red.

"Why'd you try to kidnap her?" I asked.

"Because she knows too much," Madisen said.

"She does not!" Toby said. "She doesn't remember anything about that night in Kansas."

"Even so," I continued. "When Marcia visited Mayor Holder the other night, why didn't she tell her father that you'd tried to kidnap her?" I asked Madisen.

He snickered. "She did, but I told the old man she was lying, and she's crazy after all these years. He believes whatever I say. I'm his son-in-law and I do a good job in this town. And I take care of anything that goes wrong, anything he doesn't want people to hear about."

I studied him. "Like what?"

"If his employees get into any kind of mess that'll create problems in town, or," he glanced at Toby, "when his kids get into trouble. Which was a lot with you, back in the day."

"Until you got me into the drug-smuggling business," Toby said. "That turned me around."

Madisen ignored that and stared at me, furious. "You're a real pain in the ass, you know that?"

I smiled. "So I've been told."

"Because of you stirring things up around town, I've had to smooth things over with the mayor," he said.

I nodded. "That's why you were talking to him earlier today."

"You were following me?" he asked.

I grinned. "Yep."

Madisen lowered his arms.

"Hands up," I said. He complied. "One thing I don't get," I continued, mostly to myself. "Why didn't Marcia tell me what happened in Denver? Why didn't she just go to the police?"

"Because she was scared," a female voice said.

Marcia Holder came through the door to the pasture. Her hair was disheveled, her lips formed a livid line, and dark circles ringed her eyes. This was a woman on the edge. She held a Beretta in her hand that covered both Madisen and Toby, and she looked as if she knew how to use it.

I started to talk, but she gestured with the gun at me. "Ever since you visited me, I worried that someone from Sagebrush was going to come for me. Then," she turned to Madisen, "when my own brother-in-law showed up at my house and tried to kidnap me, I knew I couldn't trust anyone. Certainly not you." She pointed to me. "But I had to come back to Sagebrush to find out what was going on, once and for all. I've been sleeping in my car, sneaking around, watching you all, trying to figure out what you're hiding."

"What do you know?" Madisen asked her.

She shook her head sadly. "I knew when Eddie and I ran away that he was leaving Sagebrush for other reasons besides just the baby and me. I just didn't know exactly what. And I thought my father was involved in Jay Overstrom's murder. While the baby and I were back home in Sagebrush, I heard father arguing one day with Toby about Jay's disappearance. And I was pretty sure I'd heard Father's voice in that hotel room in Kansas, fighting with someone. I've managed to use those things against him all these years.

"Sitting right there in my own bedroom one evening, I finally figured out how I could turn everything I knew about him to my advantage. I went to him and told him that if he'd pay for me to live in Denver, I wouldn't tell anyone about what happened in Kansas, and about how badly he always treated his family, and about my suspicions that he'd had something to do with Jay's murder. You know Father, always determined to keep his position and power in this town. He knew that if I told anybody about how cruel and dishonest he really was, he'd be finished as mayor. He went along with our little deal, and I got to live in Denver and at least be near my daughter. But after a while, I started to worry that he wouldn't trust me to keep quiet, that he'd think I would tell someone, and that then, he'd try to shut me up for good, or even do something to Gina to keep me quiet. I wouldn't put any of it past him. So, Ben, when you showed up, I figured he sent you to eliminate me."

"But, Marcia – you told me you didn't remember what happened in Kansas!" Toby snapped.

She shrugged. "Well, I didn't, exactly. But Father never believed that. And I sure wasn't going to try to convince him otherwise."

"But your father didn't go to Kansas," I said. "He was at a conference in Cleveland."

"Wait – I didn't know about any conference." She blinked hard a few times as she tried to put the pieces together. "But the voice I heard. If it wasn't Father, then…" Her voice trailed off. Her eyes went to me, then Ben, and finally to Toby. She narrowed her eyes. "*You* were in that hotel room?" She was incredulous.

He nodded. "Father sent us to bring you back. It worked out fine, because we also needed to get Eddie."

"All those years Father let me think he was in that hotel room," she whispered. "He never said a word about it or corrected my mistake."

"That's because he wanted you to fear him," Madisen said. "If you thought he was willing to come to Kansas to get you, and he'd hurt you in the process, what else might he do to keep you under control?"

She shook her head slowly. "I *did* fear him, all these years."

"So … *did* your father murder Jay?" I asked her.

Toby let out a bitter laugh. "Nah, the old man didn't do it, but he suspected Ben did."

"Shut up!" Madisen barked at Toby. "Your father suspected *we* might've killed Jay, and you know what? He was fine with that. He thought Jay was such a bad influence on you. But he's the mayor, and he sure can't have anyone know he covered up a murder. That's why he was worried about what Marcia knew, and why he paid to keep her quiet."

My eyes darted between them all. "You are one sick bunch."

Marcia sniffled, then stared at her brother. "Why are you trying to hurt me, Toby?" Her voice cracked.

"Don't talk to her," Madisen said.

Toby shook his head. "You know what? I'm tired of you ordering me around. You've gone too far this time." He looked at Marcia. "Ben asked me to get involved in the drug smuggling, and I did."

"Toby, why?" Marcia said.

"The money was a way to not have to be under Father's thumb. I didn't want to work at the plant, not for him! And everything was going fine until Jay decided he wanted more money. He got arrogant and careless, and we had to do something about it. But I didn't kill him."

She turned to Madisen. "You did?"

"Yes, our brother-in-law killed Jay," Toby said.

"You knew about it, so that makes you at least an accessory to murder. Try not to sound so high-and-mighty," Madisen muttered to him.

Toby shook his head. "I didn't kill Jay, and I didn't kill Paula, either. You did, and you even botched getting rid of her body."

"Shut your trap," Madisen growled.

"Why kill Jay's wife?" I asked.

"She knew what was going on," Toby said. "She came back to Sagebrush after Jay disappeared, and was asking questions." He jerked his head at Madisen. "Ben here was only a deputy and he threatened her, but I guess he wasn't scary enough – he couldn't keep her quiet. She said she'd go to the sheriff, so Ben decided she'd have to go, too. Eddie hadn't been happy about Jay's death, and he knew the plan to eliminate Paula, and he wanted out. That's why he left with you," he pointed to Marcia, "when he did. But we couldn't let him escape."

"Eddie was smuggling drugs with you two?" Marcia asked.

Madisen snorted. "Eddie got out of college and drifted, and had been dealing drugs. He and Jay knew some people in Denver, and they helped us with the whole thing. But we hadn't counted on the idiot dating you and getting you pregnant."

Marcia blushed and her hand shook as she aimed at Madisen.

"What'd you do to Eddie in that hotel room?" Her eyes flashed dangerously.

"Marcia, put the gun down," Madisen said in a low voice.

Marcia aimed over his shoulder and pulled the trigger. The explosion rocketed throughout the barn. The horses neighed and bucked in their stalls. Madisen ducked and swore.

"Start talking," Marcia said, "or the next bullet will go in your chest."

"All right," Madisen said, his voice trembling but angry. "When we got to your hotel room, you were sleeping. Eddie and I argued, you woke up and tried to stop us, and you fell and hit your head."

"How'd you know we were there?" she asked.

Madisen laughed. "You called Jennifer, remember? You told her you were scared, but not to tell anyone." He shrugged. "She told me."

Marcia got a faraway look in her eyes. "I'd forgotten I'd called her."

Madisen went on. "Anyway, we talked with Eddie. He said he wouldn't tell anyone what we'd done." He laughed bitterly. "You were only knocked out for a minute, and when you came around, Eddie started telling you everything. I told him to shut up, but he just kept talking. I went after him, and Toby and I beat him up. We were going to dispose of him, but by then your baby was making too much noise, and you were hysterical, so Toby took you and the baby outside. I tied Eddie up and went to look for you all. Toby had you in the car, and we had to drive you around so no one would hear you yelling and wailing. By the time we got you calmed down and returned to the room, Eddie had escaped and run off."

"Great job," Toby muttered.

"Shut up!" Madisen snarled. He stared at Marcia. "We brought you back to Sagebrush, and, well, you know the rest."

"You were going to kill Eddie?" Marcia could barely speak.

"He was going to turn us in," Madisen said.

Marcia gazed at Toby. Anguished tears ran down her face. "You were there, Toby? And not Father?" Toby stared at the floor. "I thought you cared about me."

His head snapped up. "I did!" he said defiantly. "I hated how Father was treating you. It was awful! After we came back here, Ben was going to kill you, but I begged him not to. I said you didn't remember anything, so you weren't a threat. That's why he left you alone. Because of me. And I tried to tell him that, after Eddie called the other day, but he didn't believe me and still wanted you dead."

"Along with Eddie," Madisen said.

Marcia stared at him. "Eddie's dead?"

Madisen pointed at Toby. "He shot him."

"Toby?" Marcia's lower lip quivered. "You killed Eddie?"

"I don't know if he's dead." Toby jerked his head at me. "He came into the lot, and I left."

Marcia's gaze swung to me.

"He's dead," I said. "I'm sorry."

"He was going to turn us all in," Toby said in a whine. "Marcia, I'm so sorry. I wasn't thinking."

Her lip quivered. "I can't believe you did that."

"I'm sorry," Toby repeated. Then he shook a finger at Madisen. "This ends here and now."

"What're you talking about?" Madisen said.

"You're not going to kill anyone else," Toby replied.

Madisen lowered his hands. "Try and stop me."

"Don't anyone move," I said.

But even as I spoke, Madisen lunged for Marcia. She screamed and a shot rang out, then another. Madisen jerked around, then crumpled to the ground and lay still. Red spots formed on his brown shirt. Someone shouted. The horses neighed and crashed around in their stalls.

"Marcia, no!" Toby yelled.

Then it was suddenly quiet. The smell of dust and a faint acrid bite of gunpowder lingered in the air. Marcia aimed the Beretta at Toby.

"You ruined my life," she whispered.

Toby held his hands up. "Marcia, don't."

I pointed the Glock at her. "Marcia, drop the gun." Her hand shook. "You don't want to kill him," I said softly. "Think about your daughter. You don't want her visiting you in prison."

She stood for a long moment, staring at Toby, then the gun suddenly dropped to her side and she fell back against the wall, sobbing.

"I'm so sorry," Toby said, but I don't think she heard him.

He took a step forward, and I swung the Glock toward him. "Stay right there." He stopped.

I moved over to Madisen's body and checked his pulse. "He's dead."

"He got what he deserved," Toby said.

I nodded as I stood back up. "And you're going to, too."

He gazed at Marcia, who had sunk to the floor, still crying. Then he nodded. His will to fight had vanished.

With my Glock still aimed at him, I stepped over to Marcia and took the Beretta from her. No one said a word as I pulled out my phone and dialed 911. I spoke to an operator for a few minutes, and then called

Willie. She was just wrapping up with the deputy. I briefly told her what had happened, asked her to have him take her back to the Sagebrush Inn, and to not stay awake for me. Then I waited.

## CHAPTER THIRTY

It took a while before the same deputy who'd been at Holder Farm Equipment showed up. He rushed into the barn with a gun raised and saw all of us. Then his gaze fell to Madisen and his jaw dropped.

"Is that ... the sheriff?" he said slowly.

I nodded and explained the situation. The deputy seemed stunned at first, but quickly gathered himself and moved into action. He called for backup, verified Madisen was dead, then arrested Toby Holder. At that point, Jennifer Madisen ran into the barn.

"I saw the lights go by. What's going on?" She stopped short, gazed at all of us, then ran to her husband.

"Oh, Ben," she said, choking back tears. She touched his arm. "What did you do?"

The deputy went over and spoke to her, and asked her to move away. Jennifer nodded and pushed herself to her feet. Then she noticed her sister.

"Marcia," she said in a small voice.

Marcia wiped her eyes and gazed at Jennifer. "Hi, Sis."

Jennifer dropped down beside Marcia and hugged her. "Oh, it's been so long."

The two held each other and spoke in quiet tones as Toby stared at them.

"All these years, I wondered if Ben was doing something illegal," Jennifer muttered.

"Why didn't you say anything?" Marcia whispered.

Jennifer looked around the barn. "We had the ranch and everything else. What would happen if we lost all this? How would I start over? What would I do?" She visibly shook. "That's probably hard for you to understand."

Marcia glanced at me. "Not as much as you might think."

The deputy watched their exchange for a moment, seeming unsure what to do. Then an ambulance arrived, along with an older deputy whose nameplate read "Sparks."

He spoke to the younger deputy for a minute, giving orders, and then he jabbed a finger at me. "You. Come with me."

I followed Sparks outside.

He put his hands on his hips and stared at me. "You want to tell me what's going on?"

I launched into a long explanation of what had occurred in the barn, and he peppered me with questions while other county officials arrived and hurried in and out of the barn. While we were talking, the young deputy escorted Toby Holder to a cruiser. Toby glanced at me with a stony expression as he was helped into the backseat. Then the deputy slid into the front seat and drove off.

I finally concluded my story, and had to sit on the porch while Sparks went back into the barn. When he came out, he spoke to me for a while longer, got my contact information, and allowed me to leave. He wouldn't let me speak to Marcia or Jennifer.

It was well past midnight when I finally headed back to town. On the way, I called Gina Smith. Her voice was groggy when she answered the phone.

"Reed, what's wrong?"

I stared out the windshield, then finally said, "I've got some bad news. There isn't an easy way to say this."

"Is it Marcia?"

"No, your dad. He's dead."

"What?" Her voice was shrill.

"I'm so sorry," I said lamely. Then I told her the long and complicated story of everything that I'd discovered.

It took her a long time to speak after I finished. "I don't know what to say," she said. "I ... need to call the sheriff's department and talk to them. I'll call you later."

"I'm sorry," I repeated.

"Thank you."

The call disconnected. I cranked the music, wishing it could drown out the sadness I felt for Gina. A little while later, I arrived at the Sagebrush Inn. I quietly let myself into my room and turned on the bathroom light. Willie – sans her black teddy – was asleep with the covers half pulled over her. I undressed and crawled in beside her.

"Hey," she said sleepily as I pulled her close. "Are you okay?"

"Yes, go back to sleep. We can talk more in the morning."

"I love you."

"I love you, too," I said.

We were soon asleep.

» » » » »

"Hey, Reed, I have a good idea," Deuce said as he sauntered up to our table.

It was a few weeks later, and Cal, Willie, and the Goofballs were with me at B 52s for a night of burgers and pool, my small way of thanking them all for their help. Ace had just beat Deuce at pool, a waiter had delivered burgers for everyone, and now we were all gathered a-round a table.

"What's that?" I asked Deuce.

"How about Ace and I take some gun safety courses?"

Willie was sitting next to me, and she put her hand to her face, hiding a smile.

I took a sip of my beer, and then said, "Why do you want to do that?"

Ace chimed in. "We thought if we were trained officially with guns, maybe in your next case, you'd let us carry."

"A gun safety class would be a good idea," I said.

Deuce beamed.

"You're not seriously going to let them carry guns when they help you?" Willie murmured at me.

"Not anytime soon," I whispered. "But it can't hurt for them to take the class."

She nodded. "That's true."

We dove into our meals, and then Cal asked, "Did you ever find out what John Smith's real name was?"

I grinned at him. "I thought you would've figured that out by now."

"With that generic name?" He held up his hands. "I tried."

"John Smith's real name was Eddie Lendale," I said. "After graduating with a degree in accounting, he wandered the country, getting arrested in Virginia, Miami, and then in Denver. Toby Holder said

Lendale had drug connections in Miami, and he came to Denver and smuggled drugs from Mexico."

"His crime connections probably helped him get a new ID when he left Sagebrush," Cal said.

I nodded. "Right. Anyway, Lendale ended up in Sagebrush, where he connected with Toby Holder, and they started smuggling drugs up from Mexico. But then Lendale fell in love with Marcia, and … well, you know the rest."

"What's happening with Marcia and Gina?" Cal asked.

"Marcia's back in Denver, and she and Gina are working on their relationship," I said. "Gina was initially stunned when she learned about her father's death, but she suspected him of some kind of wrongdoing, so I don't think she was completely surprised."

"It was still tough to lose her father," Willie interjected. "She took some time off for the funeral, but is back at work. She's been having a tough time, and so has her son, Ethan."

"What about the mayor?" Ace asked. "Was he involved in the drug smuggling?"

I shook my head. "Nope. Mayor Holder and Pastor Sheehan didn't know what was going on. Toby and Sheriff Madisen were very careful with their operation, and when anything suspicious was reported – which wasn't often – Madisen covered it."

"Did Jennifer suspect anything?" Willie asked.

"Marcia said she did, but Jennifer chose to look the other way. She had no idea that they'd murdered anyone, though."

Cal took a drink of his beer, and then said, "And Toby Holder's facing trial?"

"He's admitted what he's done, so I don't think there'll be a trial.

He's been talking a lot, hoping it'll help him get a lighter sentence."

"How'd you find all this out?" Deuce asked.

"I've talked to Marcia," I said.

Ace had wolfed down his burger, and he stood up. "I beat Deuce, so how about a game with me, Cal?"

Cal glanced up. "Uh, I guess so."

Willie winked at him. "It'll be fun."

"Uh-huh." Cal walked over to the pool table.

"Let's see how the genius does," I said with a laugh. I didn't have high hopes that Cal would win.

"Want to play a game?" Willie asked me.

"Sure, but you'll lose."

She grinned at me. "We'll see about that. Oh, by the way, your mother called me today. We had a nice chat."

I stared at her. "What're you up to?"

"Boy, she really wants grandkids."

"Yeah?"

She patted my cheek. "Don't worry, I told her we're not ready yet."

I breathed a sigh of relief. I want kids, just not yet. I studied the amused look on her face. "But?"

"What if we got a cat?"

I laughed. "My mother would be thrilled."

## AUTHOR'S NOTE

Detective Sarah Spillman appears in three short stories: *Seven for Suicide, Saturday Night Special*, and *Dance of the Macabre*. Each are published individually in ebook format, and are also included in the short story collection, *Take Five*. *Take Five* also includes a Reed Ferguson short story, *Elvis And The Sports Card Cheat*.

# ABOUT THE AUTHOR

Renée Pawlish is the author of The Reed Ferguson mystery series, the Dewey Webb historical mystery series, *Nephilim Genesis of Evil*, The Noah Winter adventure series, *This War We're In* (middle-grade historical novel), *Take Five*, a short story collection that includes a Reed Ferguson mystery, and The *Sallie House: Exposing the Beast Within*, about a haunted house investigation in Kansas.

Renée loves to travel and has visited numerous countries around the world. She has also spent many summer days at her parents' cabin in the hills outside of Boulder, Colorado, which was the inspiration for the setting of Taylor Crossing in her novel *Nephilim*.

Visit Renée at www.reneepawlish.com.

**The Reed Ferguson Mystery Series**
*This Doesn't Happen In The Movies*
*Reel Estate Rip-off*
*The Maltese Felon*
*Farewell, My Deuce*
*Out of the Past*
*Torch Scene*
*The Lady Who Sang High*
*Sweet Smell of Sucrets*
*The Third Fan*
*Back Story*
*Night of the Hunted*
*The Postman Always Brings Dice*
*Road Blocked*
*Small Town Focus*
*Ace in the Hole (novella)*
*Walk Softly, Danger (Kindle Worlds novella)*
*Elvis And The Sports Card Cheat (short story)*
*A Gun For Hire (short story)*

**The Dewey Webb Mystery Series**
*Web of Deceit*
*Murder In Fashion*
*Secrets and Lies*

**The Nephilim Trilogy**
*Nephilim Genesis of Evil*
Books Two and Three soon to be released

**The Noah Winter Adventure Series**
*The Emerald Quest*
*Dive into Danger*
*Terror on Lake Huron*
Book Four coming soon

*This War We're In*
Middle-grade historical fiction

**Take Five**
A Short Story Collection

**The Sallie House: Exposing the Beast Within**
Non-fiction account of a haunted house investigation in Kansas

Made in the USA
Middletown, DE
13 September 2018